The
Irish Village
Murder

Also by Dicey Deere
in Large Print:

The Irish Cairn Murder
The Irish Manor House Murder

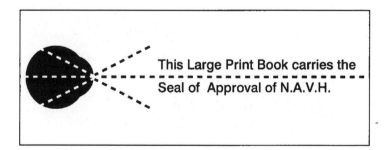

The Irish Village Murder

Dicey Deere

WHEELER
PUBLISHING

Published in 2004 by arrangement with St. Martin's Press, LLC.

Wheeler Large Print Cozy Mystery.

The text of this Large Print edition is unabridged.
Other aspects of the book may vary from the original edition.

Set in 16 pt. Plantin by Minnie B. Raven.

Printed in the United States on permanent paper.

ISBN 1-58724-843-3 (lg. print : sc : alk. paper)

To Florence

As the Founder/CEO of NAVH, the only national health agency solely devoted to those who, although not totally blind, have an eye disease which could lead to serious visual impairment, I am pleased to recognize Thorndike Press★ as one of the leading publishers in the large print field.

Founded in 1954 in San Francisco to prepare large print textbooks for partially seeing children, NAVH became the pioneer and standard setting agency in the preparation of large type.

Today, those publishers who meet our standards carry the prestigious "Seal of Approval" indicating high quality large print. We are delighted that Thorndike Press is one of the publishers whose titles meet these standards. We are also pleased to recognize the significant contribution Thorndike Press is making in this important and growing field.

Lorraine H. Marchi, L.H.D.
Founder/CEO
NAVH

★ Thorndike Press encompasses the following imprints: Thorndike, Wheeler, Walker and Large Print Press.

A Historical Note

Piracy along the Barbary Coast of North Africa lasted from 1400 to 1830. By 1518, Algerian corsairs (privateers of the Barbary Coast) dominated the Mediterranean, forcing ships of all countries to pay tribute if they wished to pass. They also kidnapped people from the coasts of Spain, England, Italy and other countries, to be ransomed or sold as slaves, as in the Raid of Baltimore, which occurred in Ireland in Baltimore on June 20, 1631, in which the Algerian pirates killed two people and took over a hundred away with them as slaves to North Africa.

In 1815, a U.S. naval squadron under Captain Stephen Decator attacked Algiers and forced its governor to sign a treaty banning piracy against U.S. ships. A year later, in 1816, the British and Dutch combined forces against the Algerians and almost totally destroyed their fleet. It was the end of Barbary Coast piracy.

1

At first Torrey didn't notice the child. It had been late afternoon when she'd arrived at the Dublin Airport after a flight from her interpreting job in Warsaw. Now, at six o'clock, on the Dublin-to-Cork bus, she gazed out through a rain-spattered window at the purple mountains of Wicklow. High on the hills, damp sheep huddled. Along the roadside, through breaks in the wet hedges, she saw flashes of still-green meadows. Wicklow's rainy autumn weather.

She bit into her last chocolate bar and gave a shiver of delight. Another twenty minutes and she'd be home in the snug little groundsman's cottage ten minutes up the road from Ballynagh. First thing, though, she'd pick up some milk and a tin of ham paste and a loaf of bread in the village. Coyle's Market would still be open, they closed at seven. Then, at the cottage, she'd shuck off her city shoes and right away pad in stocking feet over to the kitchen fireplace and light a peat fire. Already she could feel the warmth. Then she'd slip off her business jacket and unpack her —

"Ballynagh," the bus driver said, and the bus hissed to a stop. The driver looked over at the front seat across the aisle. "This is where you get off, little miss. You're to wait down the street, in front of where it says 'O'Curry's Meats.'"

Only then did Torrey see the child, who now stood up. A girl, possibly eight years old. She said "Thank you" to the driver in a voice low as a whisper, and went sideways down the steps, dragging a tan canvas tote bag. She had short straight brown hair and wore fuzzy dark-red pants and a navy jacket that looked outgrown, so that the sleeves, now too short, showed her thin, bony wrists. Slung over one wrist was a blue plastic pocketbook.

Ten minutes later, Torrey came out of Coyle's with a sack of groceries, all she could carry, what with her suitcase that, thank God, at least had wheels. It would be a twenty-minute walk up the road and through the hedge to the cottage. There was still a drizzle of rain, and black clouds had darkened the sky, turning dusk to darkness. Too bad she had only the tiny flashlight on her key ring.

Across the street, she saw the little girl still standing in front of O'Curry's Meats. She was clutching the blue plastic pocketbook in front of her with both hands. The street was empty, most shops already closed. From O'Malley's Pub, a row of lights reflected on the wet pavement. Two men came out of the pub, one staggering, the other holding him up, saying, "Now, Pa, never mind, time to go home." Another man, muttering, shoulders hunched, came from the pub, crossed the street, and almost ran into the child. He swore and continued on his way, then turned, looked back, hesitated, then spotted Torrey and went on.

Bastard, Torrey said under her breath. She crossed to O'Curry's and smiled down at the child, who tilted up an anxious little face. "Honey," Torrey began, only to be cut off with —

"My *auntie!* Where's my *auntie?*" The freckled little face was pale, the chin quivered, tears started. Blue eyes overflowed.

"Ah," Torrey said, "what's your auntie's name?"

"Auntie Megan. Megan O'Faolain."

As Torrey said later, ruefully, to Jasper, "I thought then, What a relief! Megan O'Faolain! No one's more dependable than Megan O'Faolain. Something must've delayed her a bit. My God! How could anyone have guessed!" And she had shuddered.

But now, only relieved, looking down at the tear-washed little face of the child, she said, "Your Auntie Megan's a bit late. Suppose we go to meet her. Would you like that?"

"Oh, yes!" Hands going lax with relief on the plastic pocketbook. "Can we do that?"

11

"Absolutely!" So . . . what else could she do except leave her sack of groceries and her wheeled suitcase with Sean O'Malley behind the bar at O'Malley's Pub, pick up the child's tan tote bag, and start up Northerly Road with the child to meet the late-arriving Megan O'Faolain? . . . Megan, who was what Torrey thought of as "comely," a dark-haired, blue-eyed, deep-bosomed unmarried woman in her forties. Whenever Torrey was away on an interpreting job, Megan O'Faolain "looked in" at the cottage to make sure that no mice were carousing through the cupboards and no raccoons nesting in Torrey's bed. To Torrey, Megan O'Faolain was a blessing who furnished peace of mind, for which Torrey paid her only a few pounds that she was aware Megan certainly didn't need. Torrey could tell that Megan came to the cottage because she was intrigued by the idea of this young American interpreter who spoke a dozen languages and who was renting the groundsman's cottage as a jumping-off place for job assignments in Europe. It had been two years, and still Torrey had no thought of returning home. She'd fallen in love with Ballynagh. Besides, now there was Jasper, wasn't there?

Northerly Road. The drizzle had stopped. A thin, pale moon shone down, turning the pebbles on the road an almost luminous white. But there was no Megan O'Faolain hurrying toward them with a flurry of apologies and a thank-you for rescuing her little niece, whose name, it turned out, was Sharon O'Faolain. "My mam's having a new baby," Sharon said, skipping along, tears dried. "So I'm to stay with my Auntie Megan until it gets born and settles down. My mam says my Auntie Megan lives in a big house with a *name:* Gwathney Hall. My mam says it has gardens and a maze and rooms aplenty. I'm to have a *whole room* to myself."

"Are you, now?" But Torrey looked off . . . that rustle in the bushes on the left, the moonlight slanting off . . . something that gleamed, like the length of a rifle or shotgun, though a wet reed could've gleamed the same way. "A whole room?" Torrey said, distracted. That rustle, again. A small animal, of course. Then, nothing, no sound. In the moonlight they rounded a bend.

"Oh, look!" Sharon breathed. For there, on a hill in the moonlight, lay Gwathney Hall. The moon silvered the irregular angles of the slate roofs from which rose four chimneys, wide as a man's armspread. Gwathney Hall was a Victorian country house of a type that landowners and rich merchants built in the late eighteen hundreds. It had deep and shadowy eaves and long bay windows. Lights gleamed from windows, upstairs and down.

Gwathney Hall. The home of John

13

Gwathney, the world-famous historian. Tibet, China, the Silk Road. The Digs at Knossos. And, closer to home, *The Aran Islands Compendium*. "A historical detective" is the way an admiring reviewer in *The National Review* had described John Gwathney. Torrey had seen Gwathney only once. He'd been shopping for greens in Coyle's. He'd given her a keen-eyed look and a nod. He was in his late sixties, tall, shaggy-haired, and wearing well-worn, shapeless tweeds. Villagers knew that whenever he dropped into O'Malley's Pub, it was for a single glass of whiskey, for which, when he departed, he always left a good handful of pounds on the bar, with a hospitable wave of his hand for a round or two for the other customers. He had long been a widower, and in the village had, these last few years, become subject to romantic speculation and sly whispers. Torrey herself chose to ignore the gossip as none of her business. Megan O'Faolain was her friend.

"We're here," she said now to Sharon, who stood, rooted, round-eyed and openmouthed, staring at Gwathney Hall, and who now breathed out in awe, "My auntie lives *there?*"

"Yes," Torrey said. As far as she knew, Megan O'Faolain had been housekeeper at Gwathney Hall for the last four or five years. John Gwathney must have agreed to let this child be a visitor.

But what *had* delayed Megan? Torrey

sighed. She felt a pang of hunger, a definite yearning for ham paste on country bread and a cup of hot tea. And to take off these damned city shoes!

It was then she saw a gleam of light from between the frosted-glass double doors of Gwathney Hall, one door of which, despite the cold and rainy weather, was open a crack.

2

Torrey closed the partly open frosted-glass door of Gwathney Hall behind her. Odd that it had been left open. The woods around were safe, but what woods anywhere were really safe?

She looked about. The hall was oval, and lit by wall sconces on each side of the door. A few dried leaves had blown in and lay scattered under a polished round table in the center of the hall. There was a small doorway beside the staircase dead ahead, and larger arched doorways to left and right. Light shone from the doorway on the left. Torrey dropped the child's tote bag. "Megan?" No answer.

Louder, "Megan?" Still, only silence.

"Where's my *auntie?*" Sharon said.

"Somewhere about," Torrey said. Trailed by Sharon, she went through the arched doorway on the left and came into a spacious mahogany-paneled room, elegant yet comfortable, with soft couches and lamps that cast a mellow light. A fire smoldered in the broad fireplace. A mass of hyacinths from an overturned crystal vase on a grand piano lay on the oriental carpet and sent up a sweet scent, heavy as a blanket. Water from the over-turned vase had darkened the carpet.

"My!" Sharon said, "what a big room! And look! There's a tiny light above every single picture on the walls! And that pretty foot-stool! With all those bumpy little nails."

"Megan?" No answer. Torrey rounded one of the two tufted sofas that faced each other before the fireplace. She bent down and gathered up the scattered hyacinths. Straightening, she saw John Gwathney. He sat in a high-backed wine-colored chair, his tweed-clad legs crossed, his shaggy head drooping. One dead, blood-covered hand still clutched his shattered sweatered chest that oozed blood. Blood spattered the carpet at his feet.

From the hall, footsteps. Torrey turned. Megan O'Faolain was in the doorway. But looking so different! Her face pale, and her hair, ordinarily coiled in a bun, was loose — a lion's mane of dark hair springing back from her broad forehead and falling to her shoulders. A wildness in her dark blue eyes under the black brows. She wore an oatmeal coat sweater over her neat navy dress. There were nettles on her tan woolen stockings.

"Sharon, honey!" She came swiftly into the room and knelt and hugged the child, quickly turning her away before she could see the bloodied dead body of John Gwathney hidden by the chairback. "What a mix-up! I

17

was delayed, going to get you." She was breathing quickly, unevenly. Over the child's shoulder, she looked at Torrey. ". . . so I called O'Malley's and told Ellen O'Malley to take in Sharon, who'd be waiting across the road. And to tell her I was coming. But Ellen said you were already on the way here." She took a deep breath and ran a shaky, caressing hand over the child's brown hair, smiling down at her. "And here you are! Finally."

"Where's my *room?*" Sharon said. "The whole room to myself. Mam said so."

"What? Oh. Yes. Upstairs. I'll show you. And I expect you'll be hungry and wanting your tea." She took the child's hand and drew her toward the door. At the last, she turned her head and looked back at Torrey, a look of such despair that Torrey felt a constriction of the heart.

Alone, Torrey, sickened, looked down at John Gwathney in the wine-colored chair. It had to have been a shotgun to have made that much blood; likely it had struck his heart. A killing of such rage! Beyond that, she couldn't think, would not *let* herself think. But then, after a moment: No. *No.* Ridiculous. Never mind the whispers, the rumors this past year, pub talk; there were always rumors in a village as small as Ballynagh.

"Asleep on her feet." Megan was back. "—

never mind her tea." She ran a hand wearily through her loosened hair. She was trembling as she looked past Torrey at John Gwathney's body. "I've phoned Inspector O'Hare."

3

He pushed rapidly on through the woods, away from Gwathney Hall. For a moment, hearing the crackle of leaves under footsteps on the road, he had stood still in the moonlight; he had watched the two figures pass, heard the child's voice.

He held the gun loosely. He had decided on a shotgun because that was usual in villages hereabouts, people owning a small-bore gun for hunting quail and pheasant and small game. It would look like a clumsy robbery, the thief startled by Gwathney in that tall-backed chair. Gwathney was known to be rich and careless of possessions. So, for an instant, turning from Gwathney's body, he'd glanced at a glass-fronted case with curios from foreign lands, and thought to smash the glass and take a green marble box or perhaps a porcelain Buddah, to give credence to robbery. But at once, he'd thought: *better not.* No need to hamper himself with a trifle.

So now it was done. At the end, Gwathney had looked at him, a stunned, then comprehending look. Even so, his hand hadn't trembled on the shotgun.

He smiled. When it came to the police investigation, the Gardaí would be wasting their time. No one would ever make the connection. There was no way. Impossible. He was safe.

He trod swiftly on through the woods.

4

By eight o'clock, the moon was high and a strong wind had sprung up. At Castle Moore, a half mile from Gwathney Hall, Winifred Moore was at her desk in the tower room. Winifred, fifty years old, was big-boned, with a square-jawed face and short, reddish-gray hair that she wore pushed behind her ears. Her gray-green eyes were shrewd, and there was usually a humorous quirk to her mouth, but not just now. At the sound of footsteps on the stairs, she swiveled her chair from the computer and faced Sheila Flaxton, who appeared in the doorway.

"Winifred," Sheila began — to be cut off by Winifred's fierce "Sheila! Do you realize Queen Maeve, the Warrior Queen of Connacht, was outrageously maligned! Show me an epic fable, in Irish or Greek mythology, or *any* mythology, in which a strong woman isn't portrayed as driven by jealousy! Not honor! Not any noble purpose! *Jealousy!* But when it's a strong *man* —"

"Yes, Winifred . . . But it's eight o'clock and Hannah says about dinner; she can hold off on the salmon, but the potatoes —"

"So," Winifred went on fiercely, pursuing

her thesis, "the mythical woman, or maiden, in legends, because of *jealousy,* consequently engages in horrendous, blood-chilling cruelties!"

Sheila nodded. "Yes, I do see, Winifred. *Dreadful* things. Medea and the like." Sheila shivered, not at the gruesome thought, but because the tower room was chilly, and she was slight and thin-blooded and was feeling the cold despite her cable-knit sweater and heavy woolen skirt. Castle Moore had poor heating, repairs were needed; but at least, when Winifred had inherited Castle Moore three years ago, she'd also come into enough money, though barely, to have the wretched old plumbing upgraded, so one could finally have a decent bath. Sheila hugged her chilly arms. She was forty-six and the editor of the well-known *Sisters in Poetry* magazine in London. Besides being Winifred Moore's closest friend, she also published Winifred's prize-winning poetry. Each October, she forbearingly accompanied Winifred to Castle Moore for the autumn months, bringing heavy stockings, thick skirts, sweaters, long cotton underwear and her cozy, beloved cap of knitted, hand-spun virgin wool. She envied Winifred her robustness.

"Precisely, Sheila! And outrageously unfair! Misleading! Equating strength with evil, whenever it's a *woman* who has the strength and uses it! That'll be the tenor of my sonnet."

23

"Well, it does sound —"

"I can't wait to discuss it with John Gwathney!" Winifred said, "I saw Megan O'Faolain shopping in O'Curry's Meats yesterday. She said she's expecting him back next week." She looked over at the row of books in the bookcase on the south wall. Eight historical volumes by John Gwathney. He had autographed two of them for her a year ago at Waterstone's Bookshop on Dawson Street in Dublin, where he'd been giving a reading: his *Irish Mythology*, and his best-selling *Twelfth Century Ireland*. Then, a month later, on a blustery afternoon in Ballynagh, when she'd been driving home from O'Malley's Pub in her red Jeep, she'd recognized him walking on the road, his nose white with the cold. She'd stopped and offered him a lift back to Gwathney Hall. Since then, he'd agreeably come to tea at Castle Moore, tea which, in her case, meant whiskey, cranberry buns and cigarettes, a menu that appeared to suit John Gwathney fine. So did the subject, which was the depth and brilliance of John Gwathney's works. But to Winifred's surprise, when, weeks ago, curious, she'd asked him what the book he was currently working on was about, he'd stared at her from under his shaggy brows, then drank down his whiskey and asked for another. She'd known, by the set of his shoulders, not to pursue the subject.

"Back next week?" Sheila said. "But he *is* back! Hannah saw him at the crossroads this afternoon. He was driving toward Gwathney Hall."

"Ah! Serendipitous!" Winifred stretched widely. "Tomorrow, on my morning hike, I'll stop in at Gwathney Hall and ask him to tea. Queen Maeve, or any other mythical woman, doesn't deserve to be in such evil repute. John Gwathney will be fascinating on the subject."

5

Blossom was the word that sprang to Inspector O'Hare's mind, a scarlet burst, the
blood like an immense, many-petaled flower
on the breast of John Gwathney's gray
sweater. The blast from the shotgun had
been so close that it had sent a heavy spattering of blood onto the collar of his navy
shirt and even drops of blood onto the arms
of the chair. Gwathney's head had fallen forward, a lock of his white hair lay across his
forehead.

Inspector O'Hare, a heavyset, keen-eyed
man in his early fifties, hissed out a breath
and straightened up from scrutinizing John
Gwathney's body. Nausea tightened his
throat; saliva ran in his mouth, along his
jaws. He swallowed. A sense of personal outrage flooded him. Gwathney, for God's sake!
Too terrible. What bastard . . . or bitch?
Enough. *Enough now.* Rumors don't count.
No speculation before investigation. Still . . . He
glanced over at Megan O'Faolain. She was
sitting on the piano bench, staring down at
the scattered hyacinths on the carpet. Light
from the lamp on the grand piano shone on
her dark hair and touched the high curve of

her cheek. One hand clutched her oatmeal sweater closed at the throat.

On O'Hare's left, Sergeant Bryson was on the phone to headquarters of the Garda Síochána, the Irish police, at Dublin Castle, Phoenix Park. Sergeant Jimmy Bryson's fresh-looking face was glowing with excitement. He was twenty-six and loved his job. He read police mysteries, kept in trim, and had his blue uniform cleaned every three weeks. The mere ringing of the phone at the police station set his blood racing with anticipation. Action! Excitement! And here it was. This time, unfortunately, a horror.

"The van with the technical staff should be here in a half hour," Bryson said to Inspector O'Hare, as he put down the phone. O'Hare nodded. The Dublin metropolitan area comprised Dublin City and the greater part of the county and portions of counties Kildare and Wicklow.

"Look here, Inspector!" Sergeant Bryson suddenly went down on one knee and picked up something from the rug. A shell casing from the shotgun, possibly a twelve-gauge shotgun, from the look of the horrific damage it had done. O'Hare nodded, and Sergeant Jimmy Bryson dropped the shell casing into one of the half dozen plastic sandwich bags that were part of his equipment.

On O'Hare's right, Ms. Torrey Tunet was

softly whistling "The Lion Sleeps Tonight" between her teeth. O'Hare wished she were elsewhere, but here she was, back from making a nuisance of herself in some foreign country or other. Why was *she* here at all? He'd find out and get rid of her. It had nothing to do with his knowledge that she'd once been a thief. No, it was that, as Sergeant Jimmy Bryson said, she was always mixing in. "A congenital nosiness," as O'Hare himself put it. Tenacious, too, once she got on to something, which, please God, wouldn't happen this time. Right now, Ms. Torrey Tunet's gray eyes, bordered by short dark lashes, were watching him, and that geranium color was high in her cheeks. He frowned and took out his notebook.

"Ms. O'Faolain, if you can tell me exactly —"

"*No!*" Megan O'Faolain was on her feet. "Not in *here!*" And she shuddered.

In the small wood-paneled sitting room across the hall, Megan O'Faolain sat forward on the edge of a squat tan sofa with black curved ebony legs. The room had a faint smell of sweet grass. Inspector O'Hare, notebook in hand, stood beside a coffee table that appeared to be a huge African drum on which rested a half dozen *National Geographic*s and an Egyptian brass ashtray. He was conscious of the annoying Ms. Torrey

28

Tunet, who was standing beside Sergeant Bryson, hands in her skirt pockets.

"I'd started out to meet Sharon, my niece." Megan O'Faolain's voice was low, uneven. "She's eight, she's here now, asleep upstairs. She was arriving from Dublin on the bus. But I hadn't realized how cold it was, and even before I reached the woods — I'd only got to the end of the drive — I turned back to get my sweater. I'd left it in . . . in *there,* in the sitting room, beside the fireplace. I went in and picked it up and put it on and then I . . . I turned and saw John — Mr. Gwathney. Like . . . like you saw. In the armchair."

"You'd been gone how long?"

"Not ten minutes! Maybe fifteen!" She threw out her hands in a helpless gesture.

"You heard no shot? A shotgun, after all . . . You say the end of the drive?"

"A shot?" Megan O'Faolain gazed at Inspector O'Hare. "I don't . . . there's so much hunting this time of year! Even this time of day! Hunters in the woods nearby, and the field, for birds, that . . . I hardly notice anymore, it's so . . ." She shook her dark head. "But it must've been robbery! Thieves! It had to've . . . They must have known who lives here. So many objects of value from foreign . . ." Her voice faded, came back. "They must have seen me leave. Then they'd come in and — God knows! Could they have

29

thought nobody was here? Mr. Gwathney's assistant is in Dublin. And Mr. Gwathney had been away, out of the country." She shuddered. "I didn't expect him back until next week. But he'd returned this afternoon. So they might've thought he was still away, and — oh, I don't know!" Face pale, dark hair in disarray, helplessly she spread her hands. "That spate of robberies round about. And now . . . *murder!*"

"And when you came back, Ms. O'Faolain? When you saw . . . ?"

"I called the police station! At once! But there's only the one line at the station and it was busy." She looked over at Torrey Tunet. "Then Ms. Tunet came with the child, my niece."

O'Hare frowned. "Robbery?" He shook his head. "A thief doesn't come armed with a twelve-gauge shotgun. Too cumbersome. So, not thievery, Ms. O'Faolain."

At that, Megan O'Faolain looked back at him with such a stricken, despairing look that, with an odd feeling of compunction, he added, "Still, we'll see what money or valuables are missing. There's a house inventory we can refer to?"

"Upstairs, in Mr. Gwathney's files."

"Ah, if you'll just —" He broke off as a flash of lightning lit up the dark windows. Thunder followed; an instant later, a spate of rain struck hard against the windowpanes. Simultaneously came the heavy crash of the front-door knocker. The van with the technical crew from the Murder Squad of the Garda Síochána in Dublin had arrived.

Five minutes later Torrey, alone in the sitting room, said "Blast it!" at the rain that was striking hard against the windowpane. She was hungry, but she'd have to wait and cadge a ride home from Inspector O'Hare in the police car. O'Hare and Sergeant Bryson were in the sitting room, where the technical crew was dusting for fingerprints, vacuuming up what might be revealing bits of fiber, photographing, sketching and dealing with John Gwathney's body, a sight she felt she could do without. Minutes ago, Megan O'Faolain, pale, her dark blue eyes strained, and her lips dry, had gone upstairs to check on the child, "an eight-year-old in a strange house . . ." And Torrey had nodded. She had, thank God, found a chocolate bar with almonds in her skirt pocket. She unwrapped the silver paper and took a bite. It tasted heavenly, despite the horror of the murder of John Gwathney. Murder or not, she wanted to settle in at her darling cottage, have a shower and a cup of tea, and maybe peanut butter on toast, that was the easiest. Then she'd e-mail her agency in Boston. Myra Schwartz of Interpreters International had mentioned a possible interpreting job in Portugal next month. So she'd have to brush up on —

"Ms. Tunet!" Inspector O'Hare's voice was sharp. "Where's Ms. O'Faolain?" Coming into the sitting room, he looked at her so accusingly that she couldn't refrain from rolling her eyes. Did he think she'd helped Megan fly out the window, a Mary Poppins escaping?

"I'm here." Megan was back. "I was upstairs. The child . . ."

O'Hare nodded. Thunder crackled, rain spattered against the windows. It was barely ten o'clock. They heard the police van departing, the technical crew bearing away John Gwathney's body. Sergeant Jimmy Bryson came into the library, exhilarated, face flushed, blue uniform spotted with rain.

"So then." Inspector O'Hare turned to Megan O'Faolain. "We'll go over the house inventory tomorrow — see what's missing." But the way he said it made Torrey think: Nothing's been stolen . . . not in Inspector O'Hare's estimation. He wants Megan to remain at Gwathney Hall under his surveillance. He might just as well have said aloud, *By police order,* and even added: *Under suspicion of murder.* But instead, he was smiling at Megan. "Lock up well. You should be safe, now. Even though alone."

"Alone?" Megan said. "Oh, I won't be alone! Thank heavens for *that!*"

They heard it, then, the sound of a car

coming up the drive, a car with an engine that rattled. "That'll be Roger," Megan said. "Roger Flannery. Mr. Gwathney's assistant. Back from Dublin."

6

"Inspector O'Hare! Megan! Something wrong? I passed a police van on the drive."

Roger Flannery, in a yellow plastic raincoat and carrying a well-worn briefcase, slicked a hand down his wet reddish-brown hair, which was drawn back into an inch-long ponytail tied at his nape. His freckled forehead was damp with rain. "The van skidded at the curve and almost ran into me." His glance skittered across Torrey with a flicker of recognition. They had encountered each other perhaps a dozen times on errands in the village, so Torrey knew that Roger Flannery, a rail-thin, brown-eyed man with faint scars from an acned boyhood pitting the sides of his cheeks and jaw, and who looked to be in his mid-thirties, read *The Dublin Times*, always wore the same dun-colored pants and well-worn maroon jacket, had his shoes resoled, and drove an old Nissan that was often being repaired in Duffy's Garage behind the bed-and-breakfast on Butler Street.

"Roger . . ." Megan began, then made a helpless gesture, spreading her hands.

"That business about O'Leary's sheep again? That it?" Roger Flannery gave an exclamation of disgust. "John mentioned that it's just a question of O'Leary rebuilding the stone fence. John doesn't have *time* for domestic nonsense like . . ." His voice died as he looked at Megan O'Faolain's pale face. "What?" he said. "What?"

"Not O'Leary's fence," Inspector O'Hare said.

"Inspector?"

Inspector O'Hare told him.

"What, *what?*" Flannery put up a hand and covered his open mouth. He stared, his brown eyes appalled, at Inspector O'Hare. Then he dropped the briefcase, pulled off his plastic raincoat, and sank down on one of the squat sofas. He was wearing his usual dun-colored corduroy pants and maroon jacket over a tan shirt. He ran a hand along the side of his acne-scarred jaw and shook his head from side to side. "With a shotgun! *Uhh!* It couldn't be more — But *who? Why?* Do we have any idea?"

"Not yet, Mr. Flannery." A touch of irritation in Inspector O'Hare's voice. Torrey suppressed a smile; Inspector O'Hare was edgy about being pushed. "You're presently staying here, Mr. Flannery?"

"What? At Gwathney Hall? Yes." Flannery had a lower-class Limerick accent. "That is, I live here when John . . . when Mr. Gwathney and I are working on an extensive block of research. As we've lately been doing. I've rooms on the third floor, above his study. So I'm staying here now."

"And otherwise?"

"Otherwise, I'm in Dublin, on Pearse Street."

"Ahh. And today? Why today in Dublin?"

Roger Flannery gestured toward the worn briefcase at his feet. "Doing research for Mr. Gwathney's next book. I worked all afternoon in the Ancient Manuscript Section of the Library at Trinity College. Then I had dinner at a Bewley's. Bit of trouble with my car, on the way back to Ballynagh. Needed an oil change." He raised a hand and rubbed it along his jaw. Torrey, on his left, saw that his shirt cuff was soiled, a dark, oily-looking smudge.

Ten minutes later, Torrey and her groceries and luggage were in the backseat of the Ballynagh police car. Sergeant Bryson was at the wheel, Inspector O'Hare beside him. The rain had stopped, there was a bright moon, and clouds scudded across the sky. It was so cold that Torrey was glad of her sweater. In twenty minutes, thank God, she'd be home in the old groundsman's cottage. She had stopped being hungry and wanted only a hot shower, then to bed. She'd be up at seven and back to Gwathney Hall. "I'll expect you at eight o'clock tomorrow morning at the police station," Inspector O'Hare had said to

Megan O'Faolain as they left. "I'll be wanting a statement."

"But . . ." Megan, in distress, had turned to Torrey. "Sharon . . . I don't want her —"

"Don't worry about Sharon," Torrey had told her. "I'll come over and give her breakfast. I'll stay until you get back." How could she not have offered? "What do I give her?"

"Eggs and one sausage, and buttered bread. She's used to tea, but with milk in it. She'll tell you she has ham, too, but she'll just be trying it on, so pay it no mind." Megan added wearily, "Torrey, I can't thank you enough. I don't know what I'd —"

"Nothing to it," Torrey said. "She'll be fine. We're already best friends."

Now, in the police car, Inspector O'Hare said, "I'll be wanting a statement from you as well, Ms. Tunet. Ten o'clock, please."

Sergeant Jimmy Bryson, driving, said, "Good thing Mr. Flannery is staying at Gwathney Hall."

"Yes." Torrey looked out at the dark woods.

"Protection," Sergeant Bryson said, "having a man about."

"Definitely," Torrey said.

7

At nine o'clock on the kind of crisp, sunny morning that Winifred Moore called brilliant, she took the shortcut across the pasture toward Gwathney Hall. She drew in deep, heady breaths of the October air. Ah, juniper, apples and — she raised her head and sniffed — even wood smoke. And now, ahead, she could see the smoke rising from the chimney of the pottery shop, a quarter mile from Gwathney Hall. Liam Caffrey's shop.

She stopped at the edge of the pasture. She was wearing oversized corduroy pants, an olive pullover, and on her head her dashing suede hat with the brim pinned up on one side. Hanging from her shoulder was her leather hunter's bag. It held her binoculars, water bottle, cell phone, matches and the three cigarettes she allowed herself between breakfast and lunch. It was almost ten o'clock, so she owed herself that second cigarette, right? Right, Sheila. She snapped open the bag and took out the cigarette. She lit it, breathed in the smoke and let it out through her nose, which Sheila Flaxton said was an absolutely disgusting habit.

Smoking contentedly before going on,

Winifred contemplated the pottery shop. It was set back off the road and reached by a narrow path bordered by briers. Once a dwelling, it was a stone building with small windows and a single chimney. It had been in disrepair and deserted for years, until Liam Caffrey had arrived in the village. Winifred flicked ash from her cigarette. Odd sort of man, Liam Caffrey. A potter, he'd appeared in Ballynagh two years ago. From Glasgow, she'd heard. Now there were rows of glazed pots on shelves in the front room, and next to the fireplace and the wood box was the potter's wheel where Liam Caffrey worked, sleeves of his blue shirt rolled up, strong brown hands shaping, shaping. Winifred had come across two or three pieces of his work in an outdated art magazine. But so far, none of the buses with specialty-tour groups had begun visiting Liam Caffrey's shop. Nor had he made friends in Ballynagh, though he'd occasionally drop in at O'Malley's for a beer, and two or three nights a week he'd have supper at Finney's. He was a lean, flat-bellied man with narrow dark eyes, a laconic look around his mouth, and a stain of red on his cheekbones. He might be in his late thirties and was certainly attractive to women; at least, as Sheila pointed out one evening when they were having supper in Finney's, the two Finney daughters who were the waitresses fluttered like butterflies around

Liam Caffrey's table, vying to fill his water glass when he'd barely taken a sip. But he hadn't appeared to notice.

Winifred shredded the cigarette butt. She patted the pocket of her corduroy pants. She'd made some notes about Queen Maeve to discuss with John Gwathney. She'd better get on. She took a step forward, and at the same time she saw Liam Caffrey come from the woods across the road. He'd clearly come from hunting because he had his shotgun in the crook of his arm and was carrying a brace of rabbits he must have bagged.

8

"This egg is *runny*." Sharon poked the fried egg with her fork and gave Torrey a reproachful look. Sitting at one end of the servants' table in the high-raftered kitchen at Gwathney Hall, she was sleepy-eyed but had combed her short straight brown hair. She wore a long-sleeved blue jersey and navy pants. She frowned at the egg. "It isn't cooked enough."

"Hmmm? I'll do it more, honey." Torrey slid the egg off Sharon's plate and back into the frying pan. She knew she was a terrible cook. Jasper, who, besides being Jasper Shaw, investigative reporter, was also JASPER, who wrote a food column in the *Irish Independent*, had, grinning all the while, managed only to teach her to make passable scones.

Besides, she wasn't paying attention to fixing Sharon's breakfast. She was thinking of the grotesque horror of John Gwathney's blood-spattered body. She was seeing Megan's tired face that morning before she went off to the village to give her statement to Inspector O'Hare. It would be a twenty-minute walk, at least, but Megan had still gone on foot. "Walking will clear my head," she'd told Torrey. Torrey, frowning, had watched her walk down the drive.

With the spatula, Torrey turned over the egg. She wondered if Roger Flannery was still asleep in a bedroom on the third floor. His Nissan was in the circular gravel drive. What would Roger Flannery do for a job, now that John Gwathney was dead? Likely he'd be in demand as a historical researcher. After all, to have worked with John Gwathney!

"My mam makes the yellow part hard," Sharon said. "This sausage is all right, though. So is the toast. I *like* it burned."

"Hmmm?" Torrey put the egg back onto Sharon's plate. Last night, Inspector O'Hare and Sergeant Jimmy Bryson in the police car had let her off on the access road, a dozen yards from the old groundsman's cottage. She'd gone through the break in the hedgerow and past the weedy little pond to the cottage, the moon so bright that it made patterns through the trees on the thatched roof.

Inside, closing the door behind her, she'd shivered. It was chilly in the fireplace kitchen, with its worn couch and the scarred wood table and mismatched chairs. Besides this room, there was only the small bedroom and minuscule bathroom; they'd be even colder.

First thing, she lit a peat fire to warm the kitchen. Next, she put away the groceries.

Then she zipped open her carry-on and un-packed the three things she was never without: the jump rope; a box of a dozen chocolate bars with almonds; and the silk scarf scrolled with peacocks of turquoise, orange and black. Those three. She was, at twenty-seven, sleek and slim, despite a taste for pasta and chocolate bars with almonds. As for the jump rope — jumping rope, she was positive, helped her to think, even to conjugate Italian and Turkish verbs, never mind that it also got her blood circulating and made that geranium color rise in her cheeks. "Rappaccini's daughter," Jasper had said. "Hawthorne, wasn't it? All aglow, a dangerous maiden." She wished Jasper were here now, instead of in Derry on another investigation.

As for the peacock scarf — it had been hers since that heartbreaking, unforgettable day when she was twelve. Holding it now, feeling its silkiness, she thought of her father's laughing face, his teeth a flash of white, before he'd left North Hawk, north of Boston, for a more adventurous life. The peacock scarf was the one possession she truly cared about.

She unpacked the rest of her things in the carry-on, then had a supper of a ham-paste sandwich and a pot of tea. She was in bed by eleven, half expecting to have a nightmare about John Gwathney being murdered.

When she awoke, after a dreamless night, it was six o'clock with an early morning gray light through the window of the little bedroom; and the window itself rattled in the October wind. The bedroom was cold, and she shivered, but after she'd jumped rope for ten minutes she was warm enough. Then, dressed in jeans and her mustard-colored sweater, she swallowed a cup of coffee and ate a store-bought muffin that would have made Jasper gag.

It was seven o'clock when she got on her bicycle. At the last minute, she tossed her Georges Simenon paperback mystery in Portuguese into her bicycle basket. If the Portuguese assignment came through, she'd be prepared. She always read a Simenon mystery or two in the language of her next assignment to get back her facility in that language. Lucky for her that Simenon had been published in more than forty languages.

And now here she was, in this big Victorian kitchen of Gwathney Hall, making a barely edible breakfast for eight-year-old Sharon.

"This house is *spooky*," Sharon said. "It's too *big*. When does my Auntie Megan get back? Why'd she have to go to the village, anyway?"

"She had some shopping to do," Torrey lied. She glanced at the wall clock. Quarter past eight. It wouldn't take more than half an hour for Megan to give her statement to Inspector O'Hare. "She'll be back soon. Another piece of toast?"

"No, thank you," Sharon said quickly. "Can I play outside? I won't go far." Pale little face! She could use some sun.

"It's cold out." Torrey smiled at Sharon. "Better put on something warm."

Sharon gone, Torrey did the few dishes. It was so quiet; there was only the ticking of the clock. She looked about at the raftered ceiling, the black gleaming stove, and the table that surely could seat a dozen domestics. In earlier times, white-aproned servants had bustled about in this kitchen, baking, cooking, basting roasts in the oven and on those iron grills. Smells of roasting meat, rosemary, garlic and thyme. Tureens of steaming soup carried off to the dining room. Platters of meats and covered dishes of hot vegetables borne off.

Gwathney Hall. Built at a time when such country residences contained suites, when hallways and passages led to elegant rooms with carved mahogany beds or to private quarters that might be a master's study or even his gun room.

Torrey hesitated. Gwathney Hall. Never mind the Simenon in Portuguese for now. It wouldn't hurt to have a look about.

She glanced once more at the clock and left the kitchen.

9

"Nettles on her stockings," Sergeant Jimmy Bryson said to Inspector O'Hare in the glass-fronted Ballynagh police station. "Hannah had it from Rosaleen O'Shea. Rosaleen goes to Gwathney Hall every two weeks to do the laundry." Hannah was Jimmy Bryson's girl-friend. Rosaleen O'Shea was her best friend.

It was ten minutes before eight, Tuesday morning. In a few minutes Megan O'Faolain would arrive at the police station to give her statement.

"Nettles?" Inspector O'Hare, at his desk, leaned forward. "Nettles?"

Jimmy Bryson nodded, meanwhile taking the top off the container of his morning tea he'd brought from Finney's across the street. "Megan O'Faolain had just come in from the woods, and then Rosaleen, bringing the fin-ished bedroom laundry down the hall up-stairs, heard John Gwathney screaming at her. He was in a rage. About her being in the woods, where she'd been . . . the nettles. Rosaleen told Hannah he sounded . . . well, scary."

"When was this?"

"About three weeks ago. Hannah only told

me about it last night, when I called her to say I couldn't take her to see the rerun of *Cabaret* in Dunlavin because I was at Gwathney Hall, and the Gardaí arriving, and I told her what had happened, the murder."

"Did Hannah's friend — did Rosaleen O'Shea overhear what John Gwathney was saying?"

"He was calling Megan O'Faolain names: Slut. Whore."

Inspector Egan O'Hare, after a moment, said softly, "Indeed." His desk faced the plate-glass window. He could see her coming up the street.

The new little police door buzzer sounded and Megan O'Faolain came in. "Good Morning, Jimmy," she said to Sergeant Jimmy Bryson, and to O'Hare, "Good morning, Inspector."

Inspector O'Hare pulled out the chair beside his desk and Megan O'Faolain sat down. She wore a maroon-colored sweater that made her face look even paler and a long navy skirt that came to the top of her brogues. Her eyes were heavy-lidded and her lids faintly pink and swollen. Her dark hair was untidily pinned back. "I brought along the Gwathney Hall house inventory." A weary voice. She pulled her knitted shoulder bag around to her lap, took out a folder and put it on his desk.

O'Hare nodded his thanks. *Murder most foul.* Shakespeare? Could the inventory help? He doubted it.

"Now, then." He turned on the cassette tape, and for the next eighteen minutes Megan O'Faolain repeated what she'd told him last night at Gwathney Hall. Then Sergeant Jimmy Bryson, at his desk across the room, typed it up and Megan O'Faolain signed it. She had, Inspector O'Hare noted, a beautiful hand. Slender, strong-looking fingers, maybe strong from all the weaving she'd done.

Nelson, tail wagging, accompanied her to the door. Inspector O'Hare watched her walk down the street, then turned back. He settled down at his desk and took the Gwathney Hall inventory from the folder.

Six typewritten pages. He read it carefully: three Ming Dynasty Chinese vases, six valuable paintings, including a Turner, a Pissarro and a Landseer. Blown glass vases from Morocco. Japanese dynasty bed. Pottery from a dig on Crete. On and on.

"Useless," he said aloud. He slid the pages back into the folder and tossed the folder onto his desk.

"What's that, Inspector?" Sergeant Bryson turned from the fax machine. He had just finished faxing Megan O'Faolain's statement to Harcourt Square in Dublin.

"Waste of time." Inspector O'Hare tapped

a finger on the folder. "Don't look for what's missing. Look for a shotgun. Not that she'd — not that the killer would've left it about." Frowning, he rubbed his chin. Horrifying way to kill a man. What rage to have chosen that means! He'd have the forensic report from Crime Headquarters at Dublin Castle by late this afternoon. *Murder most foul.* God only knew what rages, what jealousy, what betrayals — all had a high priority. But then, so did that other motive when lovers fell out. Ah, yes! Yes, indeed!

"Collins and Sheedy, Jimmy." O'Hare fiddled with a pencil. "Get them on the phone for me." Collins and Sheedy, Aungier Street, Dublin. Executors of John Gwathney's will. That much he had learned from the inventory. "I want to see a copy of John Gwathney's will."

"No time right now, Inspector." Jimmy was looking out of the plate-glass window. "They're here already. The plague, like you call it."

And so they were. RTE trucks, photographers, interviewers, lighting assistants in black jeans trailing cables — the lot. Nelson, that friendly traitor, was already at the door, tail wagging, smelling handouts of biscuits in the offing.

10

Up the carved staircase. Faint scent of pot-pourri in the hallway with its arched mahogany doorways. Victorian to a fare-thee-well. Torrey turned left and walked along a carpeted hall. On her right, on the wain-scoted wall, she passed a niche with a vase of purple hydrangeas that were dying. Farther on, on the wall on her left, was a gold-framed painting of a pair of spaniels curled up and snoozing. The name that occurred to her was Landseer. Wasn't Landseer the artist famous for his paintings of dogs? She was unsure.

The hall ended at a green baize door. She hesitated, then pushed it open, went through, and found herself in a narrow corridor lined with linen closets of oak, with ivory knobs. Ahead was a paneled door, dark mahogany, with a brass doorknob. She turned the knob and went in.

Spacious, comfortable, a row of leaded glass windows, a fireplace, a Moroccan rug on the floor. A faint smell of tobacco and a sharp, indefinable scent. In the center of the room was a broad kneehole desk with a green leather desk chair. Nothing on the desk but a glass paperweight and a crystal mug of pencils.

Torrey drew in her breath. This must be where John Gwathney created his historical masterpieces. Across the room was a glassed-in bookcase, on the top of the bookcase a row of books secured by bronze bookends shaped like swans. Even from where she stood, Torrey could see the name "Gwathney" on the bindings of the books.

She crossed slowly to the bookshelf: On the left was Gwathney's volume on India under British rule; next to it was his acclaimed book on China's dynasties. Then Ataturk's rise to power in Turkey. Next to that was *Ireland's Celtic Past*, the history for which Gwathney had been awarded the Skinner Prize. There were three more titles. Seven books, Gwathney's lifetime work. All ended by a shotgun blast, an explosion of blood. Torrey said fiercely, "God *damn* it!"

She turned away, plunging her hands deep into her sweater pockets. It was sad and terrible, and she had no right to be invading this private workroom or poking about Gwathney Hall. She'd go downstairs, make sure Sharon hadn't wandered off or had come back indoors again and was maybe trying to make a more acceptable fried egg.

She reached the door; then stopped. On the wall beside the door were several photographs in black frames. They were snapshots.

Some had cracks, as though they'd been treated casually, perhaps carried in a knapsack or a suitcase. Here was a smiling John Gwathney in a burnoose holding a rifle, a stretch of desert behind him. In another snapshot he wore a fur-edged hat and sat astride a shaggy, sturdy-looking small horse, his long legs almost dragging in the snow. A third snapshot showed him in a dinner jacket standing at a podium, smiling, his silvery-gray hair gleaming under the lights. Might that have been in Dublin, the Skinner Prize? She looked at the last snapshot: John Gwathney, gaunt-faced, in dirty whites and a sun helmet on the deck of an odd-looking scow.

Torrey breathed out a sigh of pleasure. She was a fool for the romance of adventure and knew it. She was like her father, that Romanian explorer, whose name, Tunet, meant "thunder" in Romanian. She'd been a skinny twelve-year-old when he'd left North Hawk, the small town where he'd appeared thirteen years before and fallen in love with Torrey's gentle dressmaker mother, Abigail Hapgood. But not even for Abigail had Vlad Tunet given up his dreams of adventure: expeditions in Alaska, explorations in Peru, mountain peaks in Tibet.

Pensive, Torrey wandered back to John Gwathney's desk. She sat down in the leather-padded swivel chair and swung slowly from side to side. She was, wasn't she, the child of an explorer. And wasn't she an adventurer herself — never knowing if her next interpreting assignment would be weeks away, or even months? She lived on the edge. She loved the risk of it. The day her father left North Hawk for good, he'd kissed her and given her the peacock silk scarf. It was the one possession she really cared about. It always traveled with her, she wore it sometimes even as a bandanna, peacocks on her forehead.

Absentmindedly, she pulled at the narrow center drawer of John Gwathney's desk. It slid open.

She hesitated. None of her business. Still . . . She gazed down at a thin smoke-colored suede address book half the size of her palm. She picked it up. Perfect for traveling. She should get one like it, maybe in Dublin.

She dropped the address book on the desk and took out the only other object in the drawer, a red leather notebook, perhaps four by five inches. A journal? She hesitated, then flipped it open. Pages written in pencil, in Greek, the poorest of her languages. With a feeling of chagrin, she dropped it on the desk, beside the address book.

For a moment she simply sat. She was a snoop, no getting away from it. But . . . what was it that Samuel Johnson had said? "Curiosity is one of the . . . characteristics of a vigorous mind." Right. So she had a vigorous mind.

She pulled open the top right-hand drawer of the desk. A bundle of papers. She lifted it out. A manuscript. It was at least two inches thick, and handwritten, with crossed-out sentences and inserts that were sometimes in pencil, other times in blue or black ink. Across the first page, in strong, jagged handwriting, was the penciled word *Final.* Was this perhaps John Gwathney's next book? She riffled through the pages at random. She stopped at a page, caught by a sentence: *Eight miles into the desert, I found the monastery.*

She read on: *The Berber gatekeeper, squatting at the gate, could not understand me, nor I him. But then, in desperation, I used the French word* chercher, *and at once I saw recognition in his sable eyes, and he answered me in French . . . It was a door opening . . . As it turned out,* the door.

A shiver slid down Torrey's back. It was as though she heard a distant strain of music.

A footstep in the hallway, behind her. Quickly, guiltily, she slipped the manuscript back into the drawer and closed it, then she brushed the journal and address book from the desk into the center drawer, pushing it closed with her elbow, and turned, smiling. Roger Flannery was standing in the doorway. He wore brown pants and a green woolen turtleneck that snugged close to his slight body. His reddish hair was combed back in its minuscule ponytail.

Torrey said brightly, "Good morning, Mr. Flannery."

He came toward her. "Ms. Tunet. Good morning." A cold voice. His gaze went past her, searched the desktop, then came back to her, questioning, suspicious. "This is, after all, John's private study. And under the circumstances . . ."

Torrey felt her face reddening guiltily, the heat rising up. "I know it's nervy of me, but I was just looking about. These wonderful old Victorian . . . And besides, to be in John Gwathney's study! Where he worked on all those marvelous . . ." Would Flannery suspect she'd been poking in John Gwathney's desk? Did it matter, anyway? She went on, because her curiosity was like an itch. "The book he was working on . . . What's it about?"

Brown button eyes, staring at her. "Unfortunately, John had just abandoned that particular book." Flannery brushed his fingers along his pitted jaw. "The hazards of creativity. Time lost, money invested in researching the project. Then, unhappily, making the wise decision that, after all . . ." Roger Flannery sighed. "A pity. But John was a realist. He recognized when one must move on."

55

"Oh?" She was taken aback. *Eight miles into the desert* . . . Regret, for no discernible reason, washed over her. She said, confused, "But . . . then at Trinity College . . . didn't you say last night that yesterday you'd been doing research in the Ancient Manuscript Section at Trinity College?"

"Oh, yes! Absolutely!" Roger Flannery nodded; his eyes regarded her thoughtfully; then one hand went to his nape and fingered his ponytail. "John already had me looking into another possibility. A remarkable mind, John had. You wouldn't find him sitting on his hands. It was a privilege to work with him."

"Oh." She felt let down. And puzzled. And she wished he'd stop fooling with that ponytail.

11

"There's a *lady* here," Sharon called up from the foot of the staircase as they came down, Torrey first, Roger Flannery following. "She has on a hat like in Robin Hood. She's in *there*." Sharon pointed toward the sitting room, from which voices could be heard.

"Thanks, honey." Torrey started toward the sitting room, aware of Roger Flannery saying, "I'll just duck out, Ms. Tunet; I've a —" when a cry, "No! Oh, no!" came from the sitting room.

"It's the *lady*," Torrey heard Sharon say behind her, as she went quickly, apprehensively, into the sitting room.

"Impossible! A mistake!" Winifred Moore's strong voice shook. She was on her feet, staring at a small television set on an end table; the RTE morning news still going on. She turned a stunned face to Torrey. "Did you hear that? Are they crazy?" Then she blinked. "Torrey! What're you . . . And who's that child? I'd have thought Megan O'Faolain . . . What do they mean, John Gwathney . . . That Headquarters at Dublin Castle has confirmed —" Winifred stopped. Her strong jaw quivered. She looked down at

57

some papers in her hand, as though surprised to see them.

"I know it's early," Roger Flannery said, and he went quickly to the Chinese sideboard. "But perhaps, Ms. Moore, a brandy wouldn't be amiss." And he picked up one of the liquor bottles.

"I am *not*" — Winifred lifted her chin — "a puling baby, Mr. Flannery. I can deal with shock in an adult fashion. As for —"

A *brrr* from the telephone on the end table beside Torrey. She picked it up. "Gwathney residence." She wondered if that was how Megan answered the phone. And where *was* Megan? She should be back from the Ballynagh police station by now.

It was Sergeant Jimmy Bryson on the phone, and recognizing her voice into the bargain. "Ms. Tunet? That you? Sergeant Bryson here. Your appointment with Inspector O'Hare — ten o'clock, wasn't it? It is now half-ten, Ms. Tunet. Inspector O'Hare is . . . uhh . . ."

Snarling, his incisors showing, Torrey thought, looking in shock at her watch. "I'm sorry! I lost track — I'll be right there!" If she'd bicycle fast, maybe she could make it in fifteen minutes. Maybe less. "Sorry!" she said again, and put down the phone. She glanced around at the questioning faces. No time to explain. "I'm off! Good-bye!"

She ran from the sitting room and across

the hall. Opening the front door, she leaped down the steps two at a time — and crashed into Megan O'Faolain, who was starting up the steps and who cried out and fell backward onto the gravel.

Torrey knelt down beside Megan. "Oh, Megan!" She looked in distress at her friend, who was trying to push herself up on an elbow, biting her lower lip in pain. Her hair had been shaken from its pins and hung down around her neck. Her red sweater was twisted under her, baring one shoulder. Torrey's eyes widened as she stared at the cruel purple bruise on Megan's white shoulder. "Oh, Megan!" she said, "I'm sorry! I'm so *sorry!* I didn't mean —" before Megan managed to grasp the neck of her sweater and pull it back up over her shoulder, saying "No, no, Torrey! You didn't — never mind! I'm all right!" Her hair fell forward, hiding her face. "It's nothing! Nothing!"

12

"A pint," Michael McIntyre said to O'Malley's youngest — Corinne — and off she went. It was twelve noon, lunchtime, folks already coming into O'Malley's Pub. Smell of beer and frying onions. Today was cod. With a gnarled hand, McIntyre ruffled his thicket of white hair. The leaded glass window beside his table was half open. He could see cameramen and press people clustered in front of the police station down the street; an RTE truck of television equipment half-blocked the narrow cobbled street. Murder last night of the distinguished Irish historian John Gwathney. At the bar behind McIntyre, a handful of lads were swapping stories about Gwathney's generosity to the village over the years. Shock and incredulity at his murder. Who could have? And for God's sake, why?

A shadow across McIntyre's table. He looked up. Ms. Torrey Tunet. Not unexpected.

"Mr. McIntyre." Cool gray eyes, mouth like a flower, and wearing that bandanna around her head, turquoise peacocks on her forehead. Swatches of dark hair, each side. Nice.

"Only so many servings of cod," McIntyre

said. "Better order it now. Sit down, lass. A pint?"

She nodded.

McIntyre beckoned Corinne over, ordered the pint for Ms. Tunet and, with another nod from Ms. Tunet, the cod with mashed for both. He took a sip of his pint and sat back, rubbing the stubble on his chin to hide a smile. Ms. Tunet. He'd have guessed it. Do dandelions grow, do cocks crow? He was in his seventies, Wicklow-born, but weathered by the life of a sailor, and every autumn drawn back to Ballynagh. "Thick as a bog with secrets, and I most privy to them all," he'd once told Torrey. "Many's a quiet little laugh I have up my sleeve." He knew the ancestry of every cottage, farmer, shop owner and estate owner in Ballynagh, and the foibles and secrets — shameful, laughable, or plain horrendous — of even the most secretive. So he waited.

"Megan O'Faolain," Ms. Torrey Tunet said.

"Six years ago," McIntyre said, "early spring. I had the sciatica, so I couldn't ship out. Megan O'Faolain showed up in Ballynagh that April. She was driving a ten-year-old Austin piled with boxes full of hanks of wool, and with a loom sticking out the car window. A weaver. Came from County Sligo. Yeats country. You know the Irish poet, Yeats? 'Come out of charity, Come dance

61

with me in Ireland.' There's a poet for you! Sligo, a bit wild, on the northwest coast, Sligo, yet worth the beauty. But Megan O'Faolain had a married sister with a handful of kids living in Dublin."

McIntyre pulled his nose. "She was maybe thirty-five, thirty-six. Called herself Ms. and wore no wedding ring. But had the *look* of having known the marriage bed. You sense it in a woman.

"She set up shop, renting next to the Grogan Sisters Knitting Shop, with an eye to tourist business. She lived in the back room and wove shawls and throws. Did well that summer — fine weather, tourists wanting stuff better than Irish souvenirs like factory-made tablecloths stamped with shamrocks.

"But in the fall, rainstorms, clouds like flocks of black sheep blocked out the mountaintops. Winds tore the leaves from the trees." He shrugged; his glass was empty, he looked around, caught Corinne's eye, and circled a forefinger over his glass.

"So . . . the tourist business?"

"Went off. Megan O'Faolain sat in that shop by a peat fire, reading old magazines and drinking cups of tea. Coyle's let her have the over-the-hill carrots and potatoes for a few pence. In the woods, she shot partridge and small game. She was a good shot. Tried fishing, but hadn't the patience. She got thin, then thinner. In November, she gave up."

"To leave? To go off? Back to Sligo? Or Dublin?"

He tousled his hair. "Indeed, yes. But then — the hand of fate! John Gwathney, back from a research trip abroad, was passing the shop and got caught in a very tempest of rain. He ducked into the shop.

"Next morning, eight o'clock, Megan O'Faolain came into O'Curry's bright-eyed and happy and ordered a leg of lamb charged to John Gwathney and sent to Gwathney Hall. Then she went across Butler Street to Coyle's and got fresh peas and some foreign-type mushrooms, and I don't know what all. At Flaherty's Harness, she got that wax polish for leather boots that some say is best for polishing furniture."

Michael McIntyre watched Corinne set down Ms. Tunet's cod, then moved his glass aside for his own plate. Fried cod and mashed, and green beans with a slab of butter melting on them.

"Then she'd . . . ?"

He nodded. "Been running Gwathney Hall ever since. Made it gleam like a Royal Navy ship. No more hit-and-miss help from Dublin claiming they can cook, and Ballynagh schoolgirls with never a notion of how to make a shipshape bed." He forked up mashed potatoes. Could use a bit of salt. "Then, of course, pub talk: the comely housekeeper and the widowed gentleman. Natural. A

womanly woman and a man in his prime."
He salted the beans. "And propinquity."

Cold wind up his back, the door opening, then slammed shut. Liam Caffrey in a duffel coat and black-billed cap went past to the table beside the other window.

"Mr. McIntyre?" He looked up to meet Ms. Tunet's gray eyes. She said, "What was he like? John Gwathney."

"A gentleman. Kind. Generous. But . . ." He chewed over a thought. That cold wind, Liam Caffrey in his black-billed cap sitting at the table by the other window. An incident. Not worth his breath to mention. Not an incident. An accident.

"But what, Mr. McIntyre?" Gray eyes watching him, relentless young woman, no backing away from it now. He poked at a green bean. "A time last month. Gwathney stopped in for a whiskey, neat. Sat at the bar next to Liam Caffrey, who was having a pot of tea. When Caffrey got off the barstool to leave, Gwathney's cane accidently slid between his legs. Could've broke Caffrey's leg."

Ms. Tunet had stopped eating. "Does Inspector O'Hare know about that . . . that, umm, incident?"

McIntyre bit into the green bean. "Egan O'Hare? Like as not, even the cat in Miss Amelia's Tea Shoppe and the fish in the fish tank at the Grogan Sisters Knitting Shop know of it."

64

13

The gleaming gunmetal Jaguar was parked on the side of the access road, close to the hedge. Jasper! Back from Glasgow.

Torrey, smiling, got off the bike and walked it through the break in the hedge to the cottage. The latticed window beside the door was open, she could hear the whir of the electric eggbeater. Whipping up something delicious for tea. It was coming on to four o'clock. *Jasper, my darling.* And he'd have brought back new dinner recipes for his JASPER column. Juggling her groceries, she pushed open the door. And stared.

"What *happened?*" The fireplace kitchen looked a wild mess: drawers of the hutch hung open, papers on her corner desk were scattered. Cushions from the shabby couch were upended. "*What* . . . ?" She dropped her groceries on the table.

Jasper turned from the kitchen counter. He had on her red-checked apron over his flannel shirt and dungarees. He shut off the mixer, grinned at her, came over and rocked her back and forth in a hug. Then he drew back and looked at her. "My love! You've had a visitor. Who? Why? I left it for you to

65

get the full impact. Sometimes, my girl . . . Been up to something? Need I ask?" He wiggled his eyebrows at her. He had a longish kind of Irish face with a narrow nose and was a good dozen pounds overweight and cared about it, but not enough. His dark curly hair had receded to rim the back of his head, though he was only thirty-five.

"*Me?* I've done nothing!" She felt indignant. "It's robbery! But . . . ridiculous! What could anyone want? I don't own anything worth a tinker's — My jump rope? My box of chocolate bars? My dictionaries? My Georges Simenons?"

But nothing was missing. Not in the bedroom, either, where drawers had obviously been searched. By four o'clock, they'd got the cottage straightened up and sat down to a tea of Jasper's warm apple tarts. He could stay only overnight. "Wicked political doings in the north; I've got to be in Belfast by noon tomorrow." He helped himself to a third tart. "I should have been a chef. What's this I heard on my car radio? John Gwathney. A shotgun, for God's sake!"

Torrey told him everything. "Only last night!" she finished, incredulous. "But already there are whispers in the village. About Megan O'Faolain. And Inspector O'Hare is honing in on her, I'm sure of it."

"Lovers, were they? Gwathney and Megan O'Faolain?"

"So they say, in the village." She told him then about staying with Sharon that morning, while Megan had gone to give her statement to Inspector O'Hare. "And I . . ." She stopped.

"You what?" He was studying her.

"Oh . . . I explored Gwathney Hall a bit. Came across a John Gwathney manuscript — the book he'd been working on and apparently finished." She was seeing the thick manuscript with the word *Final* in the strong, jagged handwriting.

"You 'came across' his manuscript?" Jasper was grinning. "Can you be a bit more explicit?"

"Well, *found.* In his desk drawer." She felt herself flush. And then she was back in Gwathney's study again — smell of tobacco, bronze bookends shaped like swans, snapshots of John Gwathney, a green leather desk chair, and sliding open a desk drawer.

"More exactly," Jasper said. "Let's get with it."

She gazed down into her teacup. She said, *"Eight miles into the desert, I found the monastery. The Berber gatekeeper, squatting at the gate, could not understand me, nor I him. But then, in desperation . . ."* Surprisingly, she was remembering it all. *"But then, in desperation, I used the French word* chercher, *and at once I saw recognition in his sable eyes, and he answered me in French . . . It was a door opening . . . As it*

67

turned out, the *door."*

"Well, *well!"* Jasper gave her a sidewise look. "Total recall. It must interest you mightily."

Torrey frowned at him. "Roger Flannery . . . he's Gwathney's assistant, *was* his assistant — told me that Gwathney had scrapped the book he'd been working on. I felt so disappointed. I wanted to read on. An Ali Baba tale? Like in the *Arabian Nights*. What? Certainly not Irish, though. Anyway, now I feel deprived."

"Easily remedied," Jasper said.

"How?" She stared at him.

"You want to finish the tale? Go back to Gwathney Hall and read on. What's the difference? Since, you tell me, Gwathney had anyway scrapped the book." He rose. "How about a walk? Work some of this fat off me, so I can pig it up at the Kinsale Gourmet Festival next month." He shrugged into his old moss-green woolen jacket. "Tonight I'm fixing us *navarin printanier*. That's lamb stew with vegetables, French style. Stuff's in the icebox. You'll have enough left for three days." *Icebox* was a conceit; he didn't like the word refrigerator. "Better take your heavy sweater, you might catch cold and I don't want my consort keeping me awake tonight, hacking like a crow."

She took her cable-knit sweater from the hook beside the front door and put it on.

The right-hand pocket was a bit weighed down, something in it. She pulled out the objects. A pocket-sized journal and a small smoke-colored address book. "But I *thought* . . ." She was startled. "I *thought* I'd swept them back into the desk." Hearing Roger Flannery's footfall from the hall behind her, she had quickly, guiltily brushed the journal and address book into the shallow drawer . . . or not?

"Enlighten me," Jasper said.

She told him, riffling though the journal that was in Greek. "I honestly could have *sworn* . . ." She shook her head.

"Your nefarious instincts," Jasper said, and his nose twitched as it always did when he teased her. Even before they'd ever made love, she'd told him about her nefarious past, the long-ago theft that Inspector O'Hare, digging deep into Torrey's past, had discovered.

"A journal and address book," Jasper said, "a bonanza for Inspector O'Hare. They could furnish clues to John Gwathney's murder. So better get them over to him. Fast."

"Hmmm?" She was turning the pages of the little fawn-colored book. Beside one address was a penciled-in date of a few days ago. As for the journal . . . she riffled again through it. "Too bad my Greek's so poor. Otherwise, with a little time, I might —"

"Do I hear quibbling, my love? Greek.

69

Farsi. Pig latin. It's a job for the Crime Department at Phoenix Park."

"Of course. First thing tomorrow morning."

14

Megan O'Faolain left Gwathney Hall and walked down the road. It was getting on to five o'clock. The sky was gray, crows like black specks wheeled and cawed. The road wound through the woods, a tangle of bushes on either side. It was damp and cold, and she had put on woolen stockings, a long heavy skirt and her old shawl-collared pull-over. Yesterday at this time John Gwathney had been alive. And today, since noontime, the press, television cameras, an invasion of Gwathney Hall. It had been exhausting. But by four o'clock, they had gone.

John. John Gwathney. Six years. She could see him now, the famous historian, rain-soaked, handsome and tall, white hair in clusters, his keen eyes taking it all in, as he looked about the emptied shop on Butler Street, her packed boxes, her old suitcase. And marvelously, the next day she was his housekeeper at Gwathney Hall and was hiring local "girls" aged fourteen to seventy to come in two days a week, so that Gwathney Hall was spotless. And then . . . and then . . . Within a month after she'd begun to cook and serve his dinner, he'd insisted she dine with him. Three months later, they were lovers.

On the road, she stumbled and put a hand to her eyes. How could she not have fallen in love with John Gwathney? They told each other their pasts, they laughed together, they talked about his work. And how could they not have felt such trust in each other? Five years. But then. *Then* . . .

Ahead, she saw on the left the path to Liam Caffrey's pottery shop. Hardly a year ago, walking past the old stone outbuilding that had been turned into a shop, she'd smelled new wood and seen a narrowly built, dark-haired man overseeing workmen who were replacing the old shingled roof.

A year ago. She closed her eyes. So short a time ago! A month later, wanting a glazed bowl, she'd gone up the path and entered the pottery shop. Liam Caffrey was at the potter's wheel, his back to her, strong brown hands at work; she could see the muscles in his arms. At the sound of the door opening, he'd turned his head and looked at her. It was a long look, with a slight widening of his eyes; then his eyelids flickered.

And now? Now she was in a state of madness, of love and despair and fear.

Standing on the path, she put up a hand and covered her mouth, her eyes wide. She couldn't ask him, because how can you ask such a terrible question? And worse, she feared the answer.

But because she could not help herself, as always during this past year, she went up the path to the pottery shop.

15

At eight-thirty Wednesday morning, Torrey stood outside the hedge and watched the Jaguar disappear down the road toward Dublin. Then she turned and went back through the hedge to the cottage where she picked up the phone and called the Ballynagh police station. The phone rang twice, then: "Sergeant Bryson here."

"Hello, Jimmy. It's Torrey Tunet, I'm calling Inspector O'Hare." Holding the phone, she gazed across the room to the hutch on which lay John Gwathney's address book and journal. It was a short bike ride to the village; she'd have them in O'Hare's hands in ten minutes.

But Inspector O'Hare was not there. "He's just left for Dublin Castle," Jimmy Bryson told her.

Dublin Castle, headquarters of the Murder Squad of the Garda Síochána, the Irish Police. Torrey hesitated. She couldn't just drop off the journal and address book at the Ballynagh police station without any explanation of how she happened to have them. They didn't, after all, fall from heaven into her lap. As it was, she could imagine Inspector O'Hare's pleasure as she tried awkwardly to explain. He would finger his gray mustache to hide his smile of satisfaction at her admitted culpability. *"So, Ms. Tunet, you went upstairs in Gwathney Hall and entered John Gwathney's private —"*

"Ms. Tunet? You there?"

"Yes, Jimmy. When will Inspector O'Hare be back?"

"About three o'clock."

"So you sat down at his desk and opened his desk drawer and took out . . ." Torrey groaned. *"Your usual thievery"* would be in Inspector O'Hare's gaze. *"Confirmed criminal. Unrehabilitated. Criminal mischief."*

No way out. She'd have to deliver the journal and address book to Inspector O'Hare personally, with an explanation. By three o'clock she'd surely have thought up something plausible. Anything would be better than what sounded like thievery.

"Ms. Tunet? You there?"

"Yes. Thanks, Jimmy. I'll be stopping in later, then." She put down the phone.

Restless. A call to Interpreters International in Boston, but Myra Schwartz was not available and would call back. Edgily, Torrey paced from window to door, put more peat on the fire, stared at her carry-on, still only half unpacked. Nine o'clock. She might as well get it done now.

She unpacked the sleeveless black dress that she wore with the dangling fake diamond earrings and hung it in the bedroom closet, ready for whatever diplomatic dinner her next assignment might involve. Next to it she hung her businesslike navy suit and white shirt for afternoon conferences. On the same hanger, she hung her man-sized Timex with date, day and world-time sweep. It was too big for her narrow wrist. But it was vital to her business.

Nine-thirty. She had a cup of tea, standing up and staring out of the window. It was a calm, cloudless day with a clear blue sky. Sun filtered down through the trees, dappling the surface of the little pond near the hedge. Calm. Cloudless. *Eight miles into the desert, I found the monastery.*

No use. Too tantalizing. And she had time. Go ahead, then.

She put on her navy parka and left the cottage.

16

"Hel*lo!*" Sharon said. "Hel*lo!*"

Torrey brought her bike to a stop on the gravel drive in front of Gwathney Hall. Sharon was hopping on one foot on the gravel. She was in her fuzzy dark-red pants and navy jacket. Her short brown hair was tucked behind her ears and her nose was pink in the cold. A heavyset girl who looked to be about twenty stood beside her in a parka and knitted cap, holding a basket.

"This is Kathleen," Sharon said, still hopping. "We play cards upstairs in my whole room. She's come to stay here every single day and night, because my Auntie Megan is busy."

"I guess she is." Torrey, feet planted on each side of her bike, smiled at Kathleen, then looked beyond her to the Radio Telefis Eireann television van parked in the drive.

"Yes, indeed," Sharon said. "My Auntie Megan is talking on the television *this very minute* in the house. They put pink lipstick on her again, like yesterday." Sharon made a face. "Uggh!" She reached out and took Kathleen's hand. "We're going to get branches with red berries in the woods and put them in the basket with oranges."

Torrey watched them walk down the drive, then went up the steps. In the hall, she went to the doorway of the sitting room. Technicians, bright lights, television cameras on wheels. Megan O'Faolain was sitting in an armchair in a sand-colored shirt and slacks. Her hair was drawn back in a bun, her lips were made up to look a light pink for the cameras, and her face was pale. She looked altogether wretched. In a chair across from her, a woman interviewer was asking a question in a sympathetic voice.

Torrey turned and went up the stairs.

On the second floor she turned left along the carpeted hall and then went through the baize door and down the narrow corridor to the paneled mahogany door. She turned the brass doorknob, and for the second time came into John Gwathney's study. Sunlight shone through the row of tall leaded glass windows onto the Moroccan rug, bringing out brilliant colors. And once again Torrey breathed in the faint smell of tobacco.

She crossed slowly to the kneehole desk. Now that she was here, it was as though she wanted to savor, in the very air of this room, what she had come to find; as though the room itself were an intrinsic part of what she was in search of.

At the desk, she sat unhurriedly down in

the green leather desk chair. For a moment, she just sat. Jasper had been right: Easy enough to satisfy herself by reading on, reading the story that had so beguiled her with the few words she'd happened across.

Smiling, she pulled open the top right-hand desk drawer.

17

"I saw your bike outside," Winifred Moore said to Torrey, who looked up from her half-eaten peanut butter sandwich in Miss Amelia's Tea Shoppe. It was almost two o'clock and Torrey was the only customer left.

"I called you at the cottage." Winifred pulled out the chair opposite and sat down. She was wearing her Australian outback hat with the chin strap and her face had a ruddy glow from the wind. "A pot of tea, please," she said to Miss Amelia's niece, wishing it were a pint of beer. She never entered a tearoom if she could help it. Typical tearoom. Chairs with pink gingham cushions with ruffled edges, rose-patterned china cups and dishes. So cozy, even a feral cat would only curl up and snooze.

"I've a favor to ask you, Torrey. Not exactly a *favor* because I'll pay you. Between jobs, aren't you? I have books with early Celtic tales — totally unfair, totally *biased*, of course — about Maeve, the Warrior Queen. And Cuchulainn. He was a child warrior who vanquished Queen Maeve when she waged war against the Ulster men to capture the

Brown Bull of Cooley. But they're in Gaelic, the books, so . . . Torrey?" For a moment she thought Torrey wasn't listening, she had a slightly dazed look. But at once Torrey blinked. "Yes, Winifred?"

"So . . . The legends say that Queen Maeve took revenge on Cuchulainn by using sorcerers to lure him to his death." She watched Torrey pick up the half of peanut butter sandwich, then put it down without taking a bite. Winifred leaned forward. "Sorcery, indeed! Legends! Fables! *Sorcery!* All to squash down women. Leads to burning women at the stake. Pile faggots around their feet. Society is always ready to hang the woman."

"Your tea, mam." Miss Amelia's niece in a ruffled pink apron set down the tea.

"Thank you . . . The thing is, Torrey, I want my group of sonnets for the next issue of *Sisters in Poetry* to tell a different tale." She grinned suddenly. "There's no moratorium on starting new fables, right?" She watched Torrey pushing around the half-sandwich on her plate. Torrey had on a green knitted cap and a swath of dark hair had fallen across her forehead. Her gray eyes, starred by the black lashes, again had that far-off, dazed look.

Winifred frowned and said, more loudly, "Anyway, Torrey, a couple of my books with early Celtic tales are in Gaelic. They might refute — *Why* you've ever bothered to learn Gaelic, Torrey, I'll never . . . However, *chacon a son* . . . craziness, as the French might well have said. Anyway, if you'd do a cursory translation?"

"I guess. Yes, all right, Winifred."

"Good!" Winifred sighed. "Life's so strange. I'd planned to ask John Gwathney his opinion on early Celtic . . . a pity. We were such good friends! Well, too late now."

"You were good friends? You and John Gwathney?" Torrey looked suddenly more alert.

Winifred nodded. "For the last year. He'd come to Castle Moore often. We'd drink whiskey and talk. I lost a *friend*."

"Oh?" Torrey was sitting up straight. "You and John Gwathney talked about your poetry and his work?" And, at Winifred's nod: "What was he working on? His next book? About what?"

Winifred thought. "Irish history, some portion of it. *Maybe* Irish history. I don't know why I thought so, because he didn't actually say. He was close, *secretive*, about what he was working on. He'd veer away whenever I got too —"

"*Irish* history? But . . ." Torrey was leaning forward.

"But what?"

"Somehow," Torrey said, "I got the idea . . . I thought, something exotic."

"Exotic!" Winifred gave a hoot of a laugh. "The *Irish?* Exotic? You must mean *romantic*." She looked curiously at Torrey. "But you're hardly inexact at words. In any language." She shrugged. "Anyway, that's all academic now. What his book was about. A dead issue."

"A dead issue? What d'you mean?"

"Haven't you heard? It was in this morning's *Independent*. 'An Interview with Roger Flannery.' John Gwathney actually burned his latest manuscript. 'Consigned it to the flames' is the fancy way Roger Flannery put it. And that 'John would never publish anything that he felt wasn't first-rate' and 'John had excessively high standards.' 'John was a perfectionist. He demanded much of himself.' Blah, blah, blah."

"Burned the manuscript when?" Torrey said.

"A month ago. In September."

Torrey, after a moment, said, "Really." Her eyes were bright. She picked up the half-sandwich and bit into it.

Winifred looked at her watch and stood up. "Two-thirty! I'm off. I've got to pick up Sheila. She's having her hair cut, as usual, with the fringe straight across above her eyebrows. Ridiculous! Looks like a gray-haired page boy. Needs a velvet doublet is all."

18

Five minutes after she had left Miss Amelia's Tea Shoppe, Torrey was bicycling up the road back to the cottage. But she wasn't seeing the hedges on either side, or the sheep grazing high on the mountainsides. She was seeing herself five hours ago in John Gwathney's studio in the green leather desk chair pulling open the desk drawer and finding the manuscript gone. And then she was seeing the manuscript with the jagged penciled *Final,* dated October 12.

But "Consigned to the flames," Roger had told the *Independent,* "in September." He had to be lying.

Torrey guided her bicycle through the hedge and past the little pond. Roger Flannery must have taken the manuscript from the desk drawer. Why? Never mind. "None of *my* business," Torrey said aloud. Her business was to deliver John Gwathney's pocket journal and little address book to Inspector Egan O'Hare. And then to get out her Georges Simenon paperback and brush up on her Portuguese.

She leaned her bicycle against the cottage wall and slid her key into the lock about the doorknob. But something was wrong. The cottage door was unlocked. She stood a moment, then looked quickly behind her at the surrounding woods. Sunlight filtered through the trees. No one; just a crackling of dry leaves fluttering in a sudden breeze.

She pushed open the door and stood on the threshold. No sound. She stepped inside and closed the door behind her and stood looking about. Smell of cold burned peat from the dead fire in the fireplace. Nothing damaged, nothing tossed about in a wild search.

Yet, with an indrawn breath, she knew. She crossed to the old hutch whose broad scarred top was her convenient catch-all. The little address book and the pocket-sized journal were gone.

19

At four o'clock, Inspector O'Hare arrived back at the Ballynagh police station from his meeting with Chief Superintendent Emmet O'Reilly of the Murder Squad at Dublin Castle. The late-afternoon sun slanted through the plate-glass window. Nelson came yawning from his basket, wagging his tail.

"Collins and Sheedy called," Sergeant Bryson said by way of greeting. "They'll be faxing us a copy of John Gwathney's will. They said by five o'clock."

"Good." O'Hare sat heavily down at his desk and Bryson poured tea from the pot on the electric two-burner on top of the soda machine and put the steaming mug on a paper napkin on O'Hare's desk, along with two fig cookies.

O'Hare bit into a cookie. He was still seeing Chief Superintendent Emmet O'Reilly at the mahogany desk in Dublin Castle. O'Reilly, in his well-tailored suit. He was hearing O'Reilly's cultivated upper-class voice reading the report from forensics: No finger-prints found at Gwathney Hall, not a hair, not a sliver of fingernail, no thread from the killer's clothes, only a bit of mud from the woods, likely from a shoe, but they had no shoe print. A search of the nearby surrounding woods had turned up nothing, not even a few broken branches where John Gwathney's killer might have lain, watching, waiting. "So the crime is deductive," Emmet O'Reilly had said, ice-blue eyes regarding O'Hare. "Your bailiwick, Egan."

O'Hare had nodded, trying to remember the difference between *deductive* and *inductive,* as though it made any difference; it was the kind of thing Ms. Torrey Tunet would know offhand.

The chief superintendent had gone on. "You've acquitted yourself remarkably, Egan, these last couple of years." An approving half-smile.

"Thank you, Emmet," he'd answered, feeling unease, hope, determination. Great expectations from Dublin Headquarters.

Now at his own desk, he munched the second cookie and drew a pad toward him to jot down notes.

"I'm off." Sergeant Bryson put on his cap. "Got to pick up the motorbike; Duffy said it was the carburetor, he'd have it ready by four." Ballynagh boasted one police car and one motorbike. On the way out, Bryson gave a small-sized biscuit to Nelson, who nuzzled it out of his hand.

The door had barely closed behind Sergeant Bryson when O'Hare heard the low screech of the fax machine on Bryson's desk.

At the fax machine, he stood rocking on his heels watching the pages emerge. Collins and Sheedy. As promised.

It was eight pages, single-spaced.

Back at his desk, he stapled the pages together, rubbed his hands, wished he hadn't given up smoking, and settled down to read the batch of pages entitled "The Last Will and Testament of John Gwathney."

Some minutes later, Inspector O'Hare sat gazing out through the glass-fronted window of the police station. It was half after five, a sudden and early dusk; dark clouds had appeared among the mountaintops. Across the cobbled street, the lights in the Grogan Sisters Knitting Shop shone yellow. The only sound was a creaky yawn from Nelson, who was again curled up in his basket.

The will. Inspector O'Hare looked down at the document on his desk. But what he was seeing was a chilly November autumn morning of six years ago, when he was out hunting for quail and pheasant on the other side of Devon Pond and had encountered Megan O'Faolain. Shotgun in hand, she'd managed only a skinny hare. Thin as she'd become, she looked a wild beauty, what with that ivory brow and dark hair tumbled about in the wind.

Remembering now, Inspector O'Hare gave

a snort. No wonder when, on that rainy day six years ago, John Gwathney had taken refuge in that bare weaver's shop, he'd come out with more than a handwoven throw! And who was to complain of the romantic alliance that developed between John Gwathney and Megan O'Faolain?

But then . . . a year — two years ago? When did it start? Those whispers in the village. Gossip. That while John Gwathney was away on research trips, Megan O'Faolain had been seen, more than once, walking in the woods with a man. No one knew, at first, who the man was. But because this was Ballynagh, where little could remain secret, the name of Megan's . . . lover? was quickly whispered about.

Inspector O'Hare rubbed his forehead. John Gwathney must have somehow finally learned of Megan's betrayal. And with what justifiable rage!

Slut. Whore.

John Gwathney at the bar at O'Malley's Pub, sliding his cane between Liam Caffrey's legs as he got off the stool. Could've broken Caffrey's leg. No accident.

Liam Caffrey. He'd shown up two years ago in Ballynagh. Had enough money to hire Sullivan & Sons to do a decent rebuilding job of the old dwelling. It was a solitary spot, a half mile outside the village. People in the arts — painters, sculptors, potters, artisans of all sorts — were choosing such spots all over Ireland. Word of mouth brought tourists down the byways to buy their works.

So, Liam Caffrey. Hard, clipped voice, faint Scottish accent. Brown eyes, dark as mahogany. Khaki pants and black sweater his usual. Well-scuffed brogues. A lean, strong, narrow-eyed man.

Liam Caffrey and Megan O'Faolain. She, with most to lose.

O'Hare rubbed his chin. Liam Caffrey — who was he, and where did he come from, bringing what interior baggage? O'Hare scribbled a note. Worth getting a report.

He took a deep breath and looked down at John Gwathney's will lying on his desk. It was dated four years ago. Aloud, he said softly, "A pity!"

"Jasper?" Cross-legged on the worn couch, in jeans and her old plaid shirt, Torrey held the phone to her ear and balanced the mug of tea on one knee.

"Jasper? Where are you calling from? The chestnuts you ordered arrived. So you owe me four pounds. What time are you getting back here?"

"Alas, my love. I'm still in Belfast, more trouble among the addlepated heads of . . . Dare I say it? Take care of the chestnuts. We'll have them glazed in Madeira, with the duckling. Eventually."

"I hate that word, it's so —"

"I'll be out of touch for about a week. Comfort yourself with apples." A full-bellied laugh. "What's with the Portuguese? A firm commitment from your Myra Schwartz?"

"Not yet." She lifted the mug of tea and took a sip. Lukewarm. Lukewarm in Portuguese? "Warm" was *quente* in Portuguese. But lukewarm? She glanced at the Portuguese dictionary beside her on the couch.

A clatter from Jasper's end of the phone, then a buzzing. "Hold it," Jasper said. A click. She waited. Another click, then Jasper's voice, "I'm off . . . What about the — Did you read the rest of Gwathney's manuscript? Thereby setting your curiosity at rest?"

"No. The manuscript was gone. Roger Flannery said on RTE that John Gwathney had destroyed it a *month* ago because it wasn't up to snuff. Figure *that* one out."

A silence. Then: "Maybe two different manuscripts? The answer might be in Gwathney's journal. You gave the journal to Inspector O'Hare, right?"

"Well, no." She told him then: the journal was gone.

Jasper's voice when he spoke held a hint of wonder.

"*Penchant,* my lass. As the French would have it. An inclination. You were born with it, my lass, an inclination . . . in *your* case,

91

toward trouble." And he added, "A slippery slope. Be careful, my love. We have many good meals ahead of us."

20

Finney's popular Sunday Special Breakfast, served from eight o'clock to noon, was two sausages, eggs, tomatoes, bacon, tea and the special biscuits made by Mary Finney, Jack Finney's wife, from her grandmother's secret recipe.

Winifred Moore, seated at the window table across from Sheila, ordered the Special, then sat back and luxuriously opened the Sunday *Dublin Times*. She was wearing a duck-hunting cap and had shrugged off her parka, so that it hung on the back of her chair. She had an hour's hike behind her, and three cigarettes ahead of her.

Sheila, who had her coat over her shoulders, wore two sweaters and her Swedish knitted cap that covered her ears. Just now, she was hesitating over whether to order the Special, what with Winifred always after her to gain. But no, she decided firmly, just toast, ". . . very lightly toasted, and orange juice and tea," she told Elsie, the youngest Finney girl, and Elsie went off with their orders.

"Sheila! *Well!* John Gwathney's will!" Winifred had folded back the page of the

Dublin Times. Her hazel eyes wide, she read the item, silently moving her lips.

"Well, *what?*" Sheila fretfully pulled her coat more closely around her narrow shoulders. "I *so* dislike when you do that, Winifred! I am *not,* after all, a *lip*-reader."

"Hmmm?" Winifred rattled the page and looked up. "Gwathney wrote his will four years ago." She went back to lip-reading. Sheila sighed and waited until Winifred abruptly looked up.

"My God, Sheila! Megan O'Faolain! Megan gets Gwathney Hall and all its contiguous lands. And practically everything else! An absolute cornucopia of . . . Megan's now a rich woman!"

"My heavens! What about relatives and such?"

Winifred shook her head. "There aren't any Gwathney relatives. He was the last of the lot. He's left a couple of minor bequests. One to the Ballynagh library, another to a historical society in Galway, and" — Winifred referred again to the *Times* — "one painting, a Landseer, 1845, to 'Roger Flannery, my trusted associate.' "

"A *Landseer!*" Sheila put a hand to her heart. "It must be worth a fortune! Maybe half a million pounds. Or a *million.*" She hesitated, then: "About Megan inheriting the estate . . . you know what the rumors are. About how she and Liam Caffrey . . . not that so far there's actually any *incrimi-nating* —"

"Look! There's Torrey Tunet." Winifred waved and beckoned.

Winifred pushed out a chair with her foot and Torrey sat down. "I'm starved. My stove failed this morning, so . . ." She picked up the menu. Actually, she had burned the frozen biscuits that Jasper had left for her. But what *kind* of a cook she was was nobody's business. She was wearing her parka and her close-fitting leather air pilot's cap from World War I, it was her favorite find at a jumble sale. In Jasper's view, she wore that pilot's cap just before taking off on some bewildering tack.

But she wasn't taking off anywhere, certainly not to Portugal. An hour ago, an e-mail from Myra Schwartz in Boston had informed her of an outbreak of a flulike virus in Lisbon. *Nothing else on the hob,* Myra had added. *Anyway, Lisbon is just a postponement. Stay cool.*

"Have you heard? John Gwathney's will!" Winifred smacked the *Times* on the edge of the table.

Torrey nodded. "Yes, it was on the radio this morning." And to Elsie Finney, "The Special, Elsie." A moment later she smelled an expensive men's cologne and became aware of a man standing beside the table.

95

"Blake! Blake Rossiter!" Winifred said, sounding pleased. "Table's big enough for four, sit down. Where've you been? This is Torrey Tunet, in case you haven't met."

"We haven't. Hello." Blake Rossiter, maybe in his sixties, had a baritone voice. He flashed a smile at Torrey and sat down across from her. A handsome balding man with sand-colored eyebrows and mustache, he was lightly tanned and wore a corduroy country jacket and well-worn designer jeans with an expensive-looking copper buckle. "Been in Brussels, these last weeks. A major business deal, then a retrospective of Belgian artists. Got back last night." He rubbed his eyes, which were pale blue, the whites faintly pink. "I'd rather have been fishing in Ballynagh."

Torrey learned that Blake Rossiter was an art dealer with a gallery in Dublin, who spent weekends in Ballynagh where, for the past dozen years, he'd had a country house some four miles past the stone bridge. "I became addicted to this Wicklow countryside," he said, turning to Torrey. "I'm a Sunday painter, à la Winston Churchill. Landscapes. Setting up my easel almost anywhere. Wonderful, these hills and the Wicklow Mountains. And peaceful."

"Peaceful!" Winifred said, "You've heard about John Gwathney being murdered?"

Blake Rossiter nodded his tanned, balding head. "God, yes! Even in Brussels, the news

. . . He's a historic figure. A terrible thing to have happened. And I read this morning's *Times*. About his will. That Landseer! Damn it! I'd known Gwathney in a neighborly way, but I didn't know he was interested in such valuable paintings. If I'd known . . ." He smoothed his mustache, made a wry face, and gave a laugh. "Missed a bit of business, I'd say. Ah, well!"

Winifred said comfortingly, "John Gwathney bought his few paintings years ago, before you ever came to Ballynagh."

"Yes, well." Blake Rossiter looked at his watch, then drew out a small black expensive-looking address book, checked an address, and got up. "Nice to meet you, Ms. Tunet," he said, and, to Winifred, "I saw you through the window, just came in to say hello. I'd hoped to have a peaceful afternoon in Ballynagh, but I've a two-o'clock meeting in Dublin." He got up.

Blake Rossiter was gone barely a minute when Winifred said, "Thickening a bit through the middle, but a charmer who's doubtless still attractive to women. Wouldn't you say so, Torrey?"

"Hmmm?" Torrey was pulling at the strap of the pilot's cap under her chin. Address book. Not black, like Rossiter's, but fawn-colored. Something about John Gwathney's fawn-colored little address book. Elusive. If she could just pin down what it was.

97

21

A scurrying sound — racoons? — on the corner of the roof that sloped down to the bed where they lay.

"Megan," Liam said. "Megan." He raised himself on an elbow and smiled down at her, then with a finger he traced along the curve of her cheek. This snug back room of the pottery shop was already dark at four o'clock. Outside, the wind bent branches, but the fireplace with its peat fire warmed the room.

"We'll marry," Liam said. But live at Gwathney Hall? He closed his eyes. Behind his eyelids, he stared into the hated face of John Gwathney. He put a hand to his throat and turned his head from side to side. "Better to sell it all." Have no memory of it, as though Ballynagh itself had never been. They would live in Dublin, a Georgian house, perhaps on Merrion Row. Or —

"At Collins and Sheedy . . ." Megan's voice faltered. "They told me John wanted his ashes scattered in the Irish Sea, off Drogheda. The Gwathneys were from there. I said I'd take them." And then, as though she expected his protest: "I owe John that!"

He nodded. "I'd go with you, but . . ." But

Inspector O'Hare and the whole village would be watching. A wind shook the window, and he pulled the quilt up around Megan's naked shoulders. She was gazing beyond him to the fireplace where there was only the wood box and, beside it, the shotgun in its usual place. Despite the warmth of the quilt, again she fell to shivering. Then: "Oh!" The word had escaped her.

"What's the matter?" he said. "What is it?" He was looking closely at her. But she could only hug her arms, she could not stop shivering.

22

At eight o'clock in the evening, in the dining room of Castle Moore, Winifred settled down to dinner with Sheila and their three guests. Winifred poured the wine as Hannah served the first course, which was crayfish.

It was two weeks after the murder of John Gwathney, but long enough for Roger Flannery, who was seated on Winifred's left, to have turned "from a really shabby frog into a prince," as Winifred later said to Sheila.

Roger Flannery was wearing a cinnamon-colored cashmere jacket with a Turnbull & Asser shirt. On his wrist was a Piaget watch. His reddish-brown hair gleamed and a small silver clip held back his minuscule ponytail. One hand on his wineglass, he leaned back in his tapestry-padded chair across from Torrey. "Of course," he said apologetically to Blake Rossiter, who sat next to Sheila, "I would have gone to *you* about arranging the sale of my Landseer, but I thought you were still in Paris —"

"Brussels," Blake Rossiter said, tight-lipped, drawing his sandy eyebrows together in a frown. He wore a loose big-sleeved white sweater and dove-gray suede pants. His tanned face was slightly flushed, and Torrey wondered if he'd been out in a meadow with his paints and easel despite the brisk autumn weather.

"Oh, right," Roger Flannery said, "in Brussels. Right. So I brought the Landseer to Beacon's. First I'd thought Sotheby's, but then I decided on Beacon's, partly because if I put the Landseer in their hands, along with the provenance which Collins and Sheedy had given me, 'an *impeccable* provenance,' Willie Beacon told me, they would advance me . . . Anyway, the painting is in Beacon's hands, Willie Beacon's, and they've advanced me . . ." Roger Flannery shook his head, marveling. "Unbelievable!" Perspiration had come out on his forehead. His face was flushed and his brown eyes shone. Torrey, on his right, smiled sympathetically. Roger Flannery, of the frayed shirt cuffs, the resoled shoes, and run-down old Nissan, couldn't get over his good fortune; it still bewildered him.

"And to think," Flannery said, taking a toasted round of bread from the silver dish that Hannah had just set down, "that Megan O'Faolain has maybe three or four more paintings worth . . . God knows what! She might be interested in letting one or two of them go. And since you're an art dealer, Mr. Rossiter . . ."

A muscle in Blake Rossiter's jaw jumped.

He gnawed his sandy mustache, glared at Flannery, and turned sharply away, bending his head toward Torrey on his left. "I understand, Ms. Tunet, that you're an interpreter?"

"And *translator*," Winifred said, smiling at Torrey. Winifred was in a plum-colored velvet shirt that revealed her weather-beaten neck, around which she'd hung a strand of fake pearls she'd bought at a tag sale for two pounds. "Torrey is translating some Gaelic for me. All about Maeve, the Warrior Queen of Connaught."

"Indeed?" Blake Rossiter said. He leaned a bit closer to Torrey, his light blue eyes studying her with such intensity that she remembered that Jasper had called the green dress she wore her "mermaid dress," the way the thin but warm green wool clung to her body. "Gaelic? Unusual, if you're not Irish. Difficult, translating the Gaelic, is it?"

"A bit." She didn't read Gaelic easily and was sometimes surprised that she read it at all. Still, there was that linguistics professor at Harvard who'd written a paper about her, explaining that her facility with languages was genetic, so maybe he was right.

"Interesting," Blake Rossiter said, but obviously not interested at all, because already he had turned to Winifred, a frown furrowing his brow. "I thought you told me . . . I thought you'd invited Megan O'Faolain for dinner this evening." He sounded disappointed. "I was under the impression . . ."

"Oh, Megan," Winifred said, "poor thing, what with all the ugly gossip in the village. Yes, I did ask her for dinner tonight. But she had to go off to Drogheda with John Gwathney's ashes."

"Ashes!" Sheila hunched her shoulders and made a face. "How *primitive!* Shuddery! Burning up a body, instead of decently interring —"

"Not at all!" Winifred grinned. "When it comes time for *me* to go to my dirt nap, I —"

"Dirt nap! Winifred! What a *disgust*ing —"

"Here's the lamb." Hannah was already setting down the serving plate before Winifred, who leaned forward over the roast and drew in a deep, pleasurable breath. "Can't you just smell the rosemary!"

"Thanks for the lift," Torrey said. She got out of Roger Flannery's gleaming new green Mercedes, and Roger Flannery went around to the back of the car and took her collapsible bicycle out of the boot, unfolded it, and set it on the road beside the break in the hedge to the cottage.

"Let *me*," he said gallantly when Torrey reached to take the bicycle from him, and he grasped the handlebars and wheeled the bicycle through the break in the hedge. Torrey followed. There was no moon and not even a glimmer of light reflected on the surface of the little pond as they skirted it and went past to the cottage.

At the cottage door, Roger Flannery leaned the bicycle against the wall where Torrey habitually left it. "Thanks again," she said. She could barely see Roger Flannery, it was so dark. She'd meant to leave a lamp lit in the cottage as a guide; it had promised to be such a dark night with no moon, and because of the little pond, the path would be a bit tricky. But she'd forgotten. As for her flashlight, as usual she'd run out of batteries.

"Well, then, safe at home," Roger Flannery said. He was a dark bulk. "I may get a little weekend cottage myself one of these days. Besides a house in Dublin. Been looking at houses."

"Really? Well, thanks."

She watched him disappear into the dark.

Inside the cottage, she turned on the lamp, then stood, thinking. Roger Flannery had offered to give her a lift home from Winifred's dinner party, but even in the car he'd never asked her where she lived. And then, in the moonless dark, he'd stopped on the access road at the narrow break in the hedge; and in the dark he'd wheeled her bike ahead of her unerringly through the break in the hedge and even around that booby trap of a pond to the cottage.

Well, well.

23

By ten o'clock next morning, Torrey had checked her finances, abandoned her attempt to sew a new couch cover to replace the worn-out, faded old corduroy cover, and had stared several times from the window at the sun-dappled trees and thought that if it were only spring, she could start a small garden on the east side of the cottage. She had also checked her e-mail twice, in case the Portuguese assignment from Myra Schwartz at Interpreters International had a definite date. So far, nothing.

The fact was, she couldn't stop thinking of Roger Flannery.

"No use, Jasper!" she said aloud. "Your lover is a fanatic." Because she couldn't let go. Last night, Roger Flannery making his way unerringly to her cottage door. He wasn't some sort of bat that knew its way unerringly in the dark, if that's what bats did.

So who else but Roger Flannery had stolen John Gwathney's journal and address book from the cottage? There had to be something in them that Roger Flannery didn't want Inspector O'Hare to know.

Flannery. If a thief, why not a liar, too?

Telling the press that John Gwathney had "consigned his manuscript to the flames."

Manuscript gone. Pocket journal and address book gone. But . . . totally gone? Torrey closed her eyes; she was seeing herself, Jasper beside her, riffling through that fawn-colored little address book, seeing a page with an address, and penciled in, beside it, a date that had caught her eye. A date of a week before the murder.

Still . . . the address. The address, for God's sake! Somewhere in the south of Ireland. If she could deal with recalling the Hungarian subjunctive in toto, then why not be able to recall a simple address somewhere in the south of Ireland? Some . . . Baltimore! In Cork. And it wasn't a name and house number. It was a place. A *place*. Forested? With meadows? Or by the sea? Should she go through the alphabet, searching through . . . She shook her head. No, the address was something romantic, at least romantic to people who build castles in the air. She caught her breath. Castles. Of course!

So, by her usual circumlocutions, she had arrived at the name.

She took a deep breath. *Stay out of it*. Not likely. She crossed to the hutch and took her road map from the top drawer.

At eleven-thirty, in a car rented from Duffy's Garage behind Nolan's Bed-and-

Breakfast, she drove south on Route N9. She was in her navy wool skirt and her heavy cowl-necked sweater, and she'd tied the peacock scarf around her head as a bandanna. The road south was uncrowded; beyond Carlow she bypassed Kilkenny and drove on to Waterford. Then she got onto the N25 and drove into Cork, where she parked and in a nearby pub drank a mug of hot tea and wondered if she was out of her mind. At the same time, she felt an extraordinary exhilaration.

Back in the car, she looked at the map. It would be through this flatter countryside, past Bandon and down into Clonakilty, then Ross Carbery, a kind of poetry in this land. Then Skibbereen, a more sea-drenched kind of poetry. So . . . ragged seacoast, old battles, old ruins, old betrayals and tragedies. At the very tip, on the sea, Baltimore.

The address. It wasn't hard to find. "Castle Creedon? Right in yer lap," a lad on a bicycle told her, and he pointed up a road going north from Baltimore. Torrey drove up the road, and then, only a quarter of a mile farther on, on her right, in the distance, she saw it.

Castle Creedon. Set in the distance, beyond a limpid lake, it seemed at first a mirage. Perhaps seventeenth century, of gray stone, and not huge, but beautifully proportioned, the castle had a single tower and a facade that was heavily covered with some kind of deep-green ivy. Ancient trees on both sides seemed to form a kind of frame.

Torrey drove through the open iron gateway, rounded the lake, and reached the castle where, on the east side, a crenellated terrace held pots of brilliant red geraniums in its notches, never mind the October weather.

"Not *close* friends," Torrey said. "But I'm helping to plan a memorial for him." She leaned forward in the soft chair beside the fireplace in the rather drafty drawing room of Castle Creedon. But at least there was a decent-sized fire in the fireplace that had carvings of shields and swords and helmets in the stone facade.

"A memorial? But why come to us? We're not friends of John Gwathney." Owen Thorpe, fiftyish, fair-haired, in tweeds and a sweatshirt, stood beside the fireplace. He had an athletic-looking body and a tanned face with shadows under his dark eyes. His tone was hard, dismissive, faintly irritated. "Didn't really know Gwathney. Terrible, of course, what happened. Rotten state the country's getting into."

Torrey said, "Oh, I'm sorry if I've . . ." She looked over at Owen Thorpe's wife, Constance, who was sitting on the sofa absentmindedly hugging a pillow. She was the most beautiful woman Torrey had ever seen.

Possibly in her fifties, Constance Thorpe had short, wavy gray-blond hair, sky-blue eyes, and a lovely curve of cheek. She wore an awful sweater set and her nails had chipped pink polish.

Torrey said, "It's just that you're in John Gwathney's address book, and I happened to be visiting friends nearby, in Skibbereen, so I thought I'd —" She got up.

"Oh, you mustn't feel . . ." Constance Thorpe said. She looked over at her husband. "Darling?"

Owen Thorpe hesitated, then shrugged. "A few months ago, John Gwathney visited us. Researching the history of castles in the area for a book he was writing. Constance's family acquired Castle Creedon in the late seventeen hundreds from the O'Driscolls, a family that had been in residence after the Creedons. That was over two hundred years ago. Constance's family has been in residence ever since."

"Oh." Torrey smiled over at Constance Thorpe. "I expect you were pleased with Mr. Gwathney's interest in Castle Creedon's history."

"Actually," Constance Thorpe said, "we'd never been particularly . . . But there are occasional tour groups, and a few historical . . . So we gave him tea and cranberry buns and showed him about." She looked over at her husband.

"That was all." Owen Thorpe's voice was sharp, dismissive.

In the gravel drive of Castle Creedon, Torrey found the lid of her rented Honda up and two jeans-clad lads with their heads bent over the engine, except that when she said, "Hey! What's up?" and they looked around, one of them turned out to be a girl. Or at least had a ponytail of fair hair. But the two faces were almost identical. Red-cheeked, blue-eyed. "Twins," the girl said. "I'm Willow, he's Charles, known as Buddy. So I'm the one that'll never have to shave. And *I'm* the better car mechanic." She giggled. "We sneaked around and heard you blah-blahhing to our ma and pa about the great John Gwathney."

"An eccentric," Buddy said.

"Crackers," Willow said.

"A kleptomaniac," Buddy said. "He swiped a relic. Pocketed it! Worthless, musty old thing."

"What sort of relic?" Torrey said.

"Sexy, maybe, in some way," Willow said. "A hairbrush."

Buddy ran a grease-stained hand through his fair hair. "All those old scholarly guys are a bit off. Too much dust in the cranium. They snuff it up their nose at academy libraries, researching stuff older than the Book of Kells."

★ ★ ★

On the sofa in the drawing room, Constance Thorpe was alone. Owen had gone out to the stables. Constance gazed into the fire. It was a nightmare, because there had been a second visit from John Gwathney. Then, barely two days later, Tuesday morning — so short a time ago! — she was alone in the breakfast room, having a totally delicious omelet and waiting for Owen to come down, when she'd heard the startling news on the radio. And then Owen had come into the breakfast room, and she'd said, "Darling! John Gwathney's been shot! It was just on the news!"

Owen had leaned over and poured his tea, but instead of sitting down, he'd taken it to the window and stood looking over the lawn. "Out hunting, was he? Badly wounded? What happened? Hunters are so damned careless." He seemed to be studying something out the window. His voice sounded tired and his shoulders slumped; he'd been off at the horse fair in Ennis for two days and had arrived home very late last night.

"No," she'd said. "That's not . . . Owen, somebody shot and killed John Gwathney."

24

"Even my mam uses a computer," Sergeant Bryson said to Inspector O'Hare. "Orders elastic stockings and such. Pot holders. Cat food. Hair stuff. Paid for and delivered." He fed one of the small-sized dog biscuits to Nelson. "Too bad John Gwathney didn't use a computer. That way, we'd have leads: correspondence, addresses, e-mail. Clues."

O'Hare said, "Right." It was two o'clock, he'd just come from a too-hearty lunch at Finney's and was not feeling strictly comfortable. Tomorrow he'd be more . . .

"*The Dublin Times*," Bryson said, "says that John Gwathney even wrote his books in longhand. *I* say, either way, bad for your back — all that sitting." Bryson squared his shoulders. He was proud of his straight, soldierly back. As for the colcannon of potatoes and such that Inspector O'Hare gobbled up at Finney's, not for *him*. He patted his own flat stomach.

"What's this?" Sitting down, O'Hare picked up the two-page document from his desk.

"Just in by fax, sir."

"About time." From the Galway Police Department. He'd sent his inquiry about Liam

Caffrey two weeks ago; were they sitting on their hands in Galway? Autumn vacations, what? This was a murder investigation! Everybody involved and the possibly guilty were already profiting by the bloody horror of blasting John Gwathney to death with a shotgun. A stunning windfall for Roger Flannery, for instance, that Landseer painting worth a fortune, and Flannery driving around Ballynagh in a green Mercedes, a fact not to be discounted.

"Peppermint tea, sir." Sergeant Bryson, grinning, put down a mug of the hot tea on O'Hare's desk.

"Thanks, Jimmy." And then there was Liam Caffrey with much to gain. Caffrey, lover of Megan O'Faolain, who'd had much to lose. Had she known about John Gwathney's will? A will that Gwathney, betrayed, cuckolded, enraged, might at any instant change? *Slut.* *Whore.* Conspire. A Machiavellian sort of word, conspire. So, Liam Caffrey.

Inspector O'Hare put on his glasses and picked up the document from police headquarters in Galway.

Five minutes later, frowning, he dropped the papers on his desk. What had he expected? Something criminal? Liam Caffrey, thirty-eight, divorced, no children, had owned a successful pottery shop in Galway. Three years ago a fire, cause undetermined, had sent the shop up in flames. Mix-up re insurance, which was supposed to have been paid by Caffrey's ex-wife, but wasn't. Malice? Forgetfulness? Anybody's guess. In any event, it wiped Caffrey out. Two months later Caffrey, with nothing more than a few write-ups on his pottery-making in art magazines, had appeared in Ballynagh.

"You read the fax?" O'Hare said to Sergeant Bryson.

"Yes, sir, when it came in. But where'd Liam Caffrey get the money to pay Sullivan to fix up the old Dugan place, put on a new roof?"

O'Hare said slowly, "People have friends. Or Caffrey could get credit and hang on for a while. Swinging by his teeth, for all anyone knows. Casting about for . . . God knows what. A fortune?"

Sergeant Bryson was eating one of the fig cookies from the box on top of the soda machine beside the door. "Oh? I saw *her,* Megan O'Faolain, coming out of Grogan Sisters Knitting Shop with that little niece, Sharon; she'd just bought her new mittens with kittens on the backs. 'A handsome woman,' my mam would call Megan O'Faolain. But gone pale, lately, not her usual high color. RTE reporters and all, lawyers' meetings in Dublin. Taking Gwathney's ashes to Drogheda. Knocked the wind out. But still handsome."

O'Hare nodded. Handsome. Megan O'Faolain was also now the richest woman in

Ballynagh, likely the richest woman in this corner of Wicklow. And with a lover, besides.

O'Hare rubbed his chin. Michael Fogarty's report. In the file across the room was Fogarty's interview of two weeks ago with Liam Caffrey. Fogarty had been one of the Murder Squad from the Crime Division of the Garda Síochána in Dublin, one of the four Gardaí who had inched over the surrounding woods and had questioned nearby residents who might have seen or heard someone lurking about in the fields or woods the evening John Gwathney was murdered. A lost button off a jacket, a footprint, even the shotgun itself.

The nearest resident to Gwathney Hall was Liam Caffrey, who, questioned, had said that, in fact, around six o'clock he'd heard someone go past on the road. Not voices, just footsteps. "The road near the path is pebbly, makes a crunch," Caffrey had told Fogarty. "Definitely heavy footsteps, though, or I wouldn't have heard."

Inspector O'Hare rubbed his chin. Heavy footsteps. But it had been a chilly night. Was Liam Caffrey so warm-blooded that he had the windows open, to have heard all the way down the path to the road? Moreover, Dugan's old dwelling was fieldstone, and Brian Sullivan and his sons had made a tight roof.

"It figures," O'Hare said aloud, cupping the mug of tea, feeling the warmth.

"Figures, sir?"

"I'm thinking that Roger Flannery's windfall from John Gwathney's death is due to his being nothing more than a lucky bastard. He's no murderer."

"Sir? I thought we were talking about Liam Caffrey."

"We are, Jimmy. We're talking about Liam Caffrey and Megan O'Faolain."

25

"My love!"

"Where *are* you? Jasper, I've been wanting . . . I need your perspicacious —"

"What big words, you have, Grandmother."

Holding the phone, Torrey tried to slide the biscuits into the oven, but the pan slipped and they fell on the floor. So much for that. They probably wouldn't have risen, anyway, they almost never did. It was four o'clock. She'd have bread and butter with her tea. Juggling the phone, she picked up the biscuits, dumped them in the trash, and sat down at the kitchen table. "Tell me about you, first. Such as when do I see you?"

"Not till Doomsday. Translate that to in almost two weeks. Series of sober meetings going on here in Belfast. Morning coats, grave faces, 'significant progress,' the press says. Likely in the next millennium. Sorry, my love, but there it is. Now I'm ready to be perspicacious."

She told him then, first, that she was sure Roger Flannery had stolen the pocket journal and address book from the cottage. "Find out about Flannery, will you, Jasper. He has something to hide and he's come into a fortune. That Landseer."

"Right."

Then she told him about having gone to Castle Creedon on the south coast, and the strangeness of her visit. "A hairbrush! The twins told me that John Gwathney swiped an old hairbrush. Their parents had shown him about, he said he'd come to Castle Creedon because he was interested in researching historical castles in Cork. I expect they showed him relics and . . . well, God knows what. Stuff in glass cases? *Heirlooms?*" She paused at a sudden thought. "Maybe his visit was about a *later* historical book he was planning. On Ireland. Because it couldn't be . . ." She stopped. *Eight miles into the desert . . .*

Jasper said, "I'll check out Roger Flannery. Take care of the figs."

In the narrow front room of his shabby flat on Pearse Street, Roger Flannery used his new slender silver pen to sign the check for the initial payment on the elegant Georgian house. It was on Boylston Street in Ballsbridge, that prestigious quarter of Dublin. White stone, paneled front door, a fanlight. He would drop the check off at Haines, Ltd., this afternoon instead of trusting it to the post.

"We'll be living there next month," he said to Cherry, who was coming into the front room, barefoot and wearing only his new maroon silk robe. She had just showered. She loved to wear his things. Which was fine. Whatever Cherry did was fine. And now, finally, she was leaving Willy for him. He had thought it would never happen. Saucy face, auburn hair. And that cruel limp, courtesy of Willy. In the elegant house in Ballsbridge they would have a drawing room: sofas with plump cushions; a graceful fireplace; and above the fireplace, lit by a subdued light, a copy of the Landseer. His legacy. For remembrance.

"But *when?*" Cherry said. "When can we move in?"

"Month or two's my guess." Meantime, no reason to shift his files and other belongings from his third-floor quarters at Gwathney Hall to this minuscule flat, which was already overflowing with Cherry's things. Megan O'Faolain wouldn't begrudge him his old quarters. She had too much else to concern her. "Poor Megan," he said under his breath. He frowned, feeling a stab of sympathy, remembering how Megan had brought him up snacks and soup on many a late night when he'd had to organize his research for John Gwathney by morning. And then, those other things, the ugly, secret things . . . But what good was his sympathy for Megan now? "No good at all," he said aloud.

"What?" Cherry tipped her head at him.

"Nothing, I was just . . . What do you say

to the ribs of lamb at the Shelbourne for dinner? You liked them last week. Shall I make a reservation?" The very words, *make a reservation*, made him abruptly give a breathless little laugh, so that Cherry looked at him in surprise.

26

"You're a service to the female sex," Winifred said to Torrey, and she smacked a hand heartily down on the translated pages. "The Warrior Queen Maeve! None of that Joan of Arc drivel, fighting *men's* wars! A shot of brandy in your tea, Torrey?"

"Absolutely." It was only ten o'clock in the morning, but her fingertips were still frozen; she'd come on her bicycle, and she and Winifred were in the chilly tower room of Castle Moore, where Winifred wrote her modern works on a computer and her medieval sonnets, rondels, villanelles and ballads with a feather pen. On the desk, the battered electric hot-water pot steamed.

Winifred wore her usual khaki pants and flannel shirt. But around her neck was an incredibly beautiful knitted apricot-colored scarf that looked soft as thistledown, weightless as gossamer.

"Like my scarf?" Winifred said, catching Torrey's glance. "Cost a packet, no doubt. Not mine, but I couldn't resist . . . It's Megan O'Faolain's. Had her to tea, and she forgot it. Must be spending her fortune, as witness this priceless bit of fluff."

Winifred unwound the scarf from her neck. "Got to return it to Megan before I wear it out. Tempting. Did you know that the Moores, my branch, anyway, were a light-fingered lot?" She ran a hand through her rough gray hair and looked at the clock. "Fifteen minutes until my second cigarette. Then the sonnet, overdue, for *Sisters in Poetry*. Sheila may *look* a weakling, but she's a galley slave-master about deadlines . . . You wouldn't care to return Megan's scarf for me? Or would you?"

Megan said, "Thanks, Torrey. I missed it, but I was just too . . ." She held the soft apricot-colored scarf in both hands, looking down at it.

Just too . . . *tired,* Torrey thought. A weak sunlight came through the mullioned sitting room windows at Gwathney Hall. Megan was thinner; faint hollows in her cheeks made her dark blue eyes look even larger. She wore a high-necked black cashmere sweater and a long violet woolen skirt. Talking, she nervously kept scooping her dark hair behind her ears. "Sharon is somewhere about. I'll be keeping her at Gwathney Hall for a bit. Her mother hasn't come through the baby's delivery very well. So — anyway . . . Can you stay for lunch?" And then: "Who's *that?*" — for the reflection of a car glittered across the windowpanes. Then came the muffled sound of a car door slamming.

★ ★ ★

Blake Rossiter, wrapped in a suede duffel coat the same shade as his sandy mustache, and wearing a brimmed cap on his handsome balding head, said, "No, thanks, I won't sit down. Sorry to burst in on you, Ms. O'Faolain. Glad to find Ms. Tunet here, though." He flashed an easy smile at Torrey. "Haven't seen you since Winifred's dinner party." He turned back to Megan.

"Roger Flannery mentioned at that dinner party that John Gwathney's estate contained two or three more paintings. I merely want to let you know, Ms. O'Faolain, that if in the future you should be interested in selling, I'd appreciate it if you'd let me know. As a dealer, I deal constantly with private collectors, collectors who can afford . . . So if, at any time . . ." Blake Rossiter drew a card from his jacket pocket. "My place in Ballynagh and my office in Dublin."

Megan, holding the card, said, "Thank you, Mr. Rossiter. I've so far given no thought to . . . But thank you."

Torrey waited by the window while Megan saw Blake Rossiter out and came back.

"Nice-enough man," Megan said. "But I'd feel obligated to sell any paintings through Mr. Bendersford, if at all, and not through Mr. —" She glanced at the card she still held. "Through Mr. Rossiter. Not that I've thought of disposing of anything in Gwathney

123

Hall as yet. I . . . I don't, I haven't . . . I'm not sure of my future plans." Color came up in her pale face.

"Why through Mr. Bendersford?" Torrey said, wondering who Bendersford was.

"I guess because John had bought the Landseer years ago through Bendersford. He's a dealer in Dublin. They were friendly, John and Bendersford. I met him only once. Maybe two months ago? He stopped at Gwathney Hall on his way to Waterford, wanting John to autograph a copy of *The Silk Road* for his seventeen-year-old nephew, who is a big fan of John's work." Megan was smiling. "That day, John was elated about the way his new book was coming along. He was . . . hospitable, happy, expansive. Not like . . . well, sometimes, lately."

"That's nice," Torrey said tentatively.

"I made a lobster lunch. It was lovely, we had a white wine. I was happy to see John so relaxed. So buoyant. Because lately . . ." She closed her eyes.

Because lately you were in bed with Liam Caffrey in the pottery shop. Torrey almost said it aloud.

"Anyway," Megan said, "I haven't even begun to take inventory of Gwathney Hall. I'll do that before we . . . before I . . ." She lifted a hand and rubbed her forehead. "Anyway . . . Can you stay for lunch?"

"Thanks, but I've got to get on." Torrey

zipped up her jacket and felt for her gloves. Megan accompanied her into the hall.

At the door, Torrey, looking at Megan's thin face, said impulsively, "If there's anything I can do, I'm just a bicycle ride away and marking time between jobs."

Megan said, "Oh, Torrey! Would you? Could you? Tomorrow I have to go to Dublin, to the lawyers. And Kathleen, the village girl who's taking care of Sharon, sort of a nanny — Kathleen is supposed to go to her Weight Watchers group in the village, ten to noon. Maybe you could take over? Two hours."

"Of course, Megan." It wasn't Newton's apple falling into her lap, but it would suffice.

At three-thirty, Torrey's phone rang. She stabbed the needle into the pea-green corduroy in her fresh attempt to sew a new couch cover and picked up the phone from the cushion beside her.

"Torrey? Calling from inside the lion's mouth. That is to say, Belfast. Did the research, my love, as per your request."

"Jasper, *really?* So soon? You truly are —"

"And even sent you a box of Malachy's Mixed-Berry Preserves, only available here if you give up your virginity to a dragon. Now, here's what I got:

"Roger Flannery, aged twenty-nine.

Flannery was lifted out of the Limerick gutter by John Gwathney, his problem being alcohol, no home or family. That was eight years ago. Typical Gwathney act when in his Good Samaritan mode. Shaped Flannery up, God knows how. Discovered that Flannery at fifteen had won a history scholarship, but the scholarship went down the drain when young Flannery discovered malt and hops. Hah! Gwathney rehabilitated the lad via some strange alchemy — stern kindness and discipline? A good dose of AA? And Flannery became Gwathney's research assistant. Researcher on Gwathney's last three books."

"What about money? Flannery's salary?"

"Good. Good enough. But God knows what Flannery spent it on, what with his old car and his cheap flat on Pearse Street. No booze, so that's not it. Maybe saving it up for his headstone, ha-ha?" A pause. Then Jasper's voice, serious:

"So that's that, my love. But I'm thinking of what Miller says in *The Official Rules*. Worth your paying attention to."

Torrey glanced over at the hutch where Jasper's copy of his beloved Dickson's *The Official Rules* stood beside her half dozen dictionaries. "Miller? Says what?"

"Says 'You can't tell how deep a puddle is until you step into it.' "

27

At nine-thirty, Friday morning, Torrey bicycled up the drive to Gwathney Hall.

Kathleen, Sharon's nanny, was waiting on the stone steps. She was plump as a pigeon and was wearing a rust-colored overall a size too small, and an unzipped windbreaker. An outsized shoulder bag hung from one shoulder. She had a wide, pretty face and short hair of the smallest blond ringlets Torrey had ever seen.

"I've made Sharon's lunch, Ms. Tunet," Kathleen said the instant Torrey braked her bike to a stop. She was already inching off to a Toyota parked in the drive. "Ham with peas, it's in the fridge and only needs heating up, and there's strawberry ice cream. So I'll be off." She hitched her shoulder bag farther up her shoulder. "Sharon's in her room looking at her show on the telly. Second floor, above the drawing room." Then, awkwardly: "I do appreciate it, Ms. Tunet."

"That's all right. Glad to."

Torrey watched the Toyota disappear down the drive. Two hours. She had at least two hours. Whistling under her breath, she ran up the steps of Gwathney Hall.

On the second floor, she went past a door on the left which bore an orange-crayoned sign: *Do Not Disturb on Pain of Death.* Squeaky animated voices emanated from the room. At the end of the hall, she went up a narrower staircase to the third floor.

At the far end of the hall, she found Roger Flannery's quarters. The moment she opened the door, she smelled the expensive cologne he'd worn at Winifred Moore's dinner party. So he still indeed used these rooms, as well as his flat in Dublin. She crossed her fingers and looked about. A comfortable sitting room with, at the far end, an alcove with a solid walnut bed and a marble-topped dresser. Through a half-open door in the alcove, she glimpsed a wainscoted bathroom with a claw-legged bathtub.

"With intent to steal," she said softly. But she was no longer a thief. She was in Roger Flannery's rooms to get back the journal and address book that she was sure he'd stolen from her. She'd deliver them to Inspector O'Hare. The journal might shed light on who had reason to kill John Gwathney. Possibly that's why Roger Flannery had stolen it. So . . .

A half hour later, frustrated, she sank down on the edge of Flannery's bed. In the bedroom, she'd gone carefully through the bureau drawers, then through the clothes in his closet. In the bathroom, the cabinets had revealed nothing. She had even leafed through the magazines on the side table beside the couch in the sitting room. The drawers of the desk under the window had yielded nothing. Neither had the state-of-the-art office file beside the desk. Flannery had either destroyed the journal or it was in his flat in Dublin.

She sneezed. That expensive scent, cologne or perfume, whichever it was, she was allergic to it. She sneezed again. On the bureau, beside a silver-framed photograph of a saucy-faced young woman, was a box of tissues.

Of course. Sneezing again, she got up and crossed to the bureau. She lifted out the tissues. And there it was. The journal.

She took it out. But the address book was not there. Instead, under the journal, were three little packets: cellophane envelopes of what looked like white flour.

Flour. But of course not flour. Torrey held one of the packets. So that's where Roger Flannery's money went. Flannery's run-down heels, his wretched car always in repair at Duffy's Garage, his worn shirt cuffs.

She put the three little packets back under the face tissues, then shoved John Gwathney's journal deep, *deep* into her jeans pocket. She sneezed again, blew her nose on a tissue, and left the room.

Wanting to think, she took the back road.

It circumvented the village; a seldom-used road, she'd pass only Healey's farm and its pasture land. She'd likely meet no one, and she'd reach the access road only a few hundred yards north of the cottage.

Drugs. Little plastic bags worth God knows what. Roger Flannery. Looking at him, you couldn't have guessed. But the journal! With a feeling of anticipation, she ran a hand along her jeans pocket, feeling the journal's rectangular outline. First thing at the cottage, she'd settle down with a mug of tea and the journal. First —

The bike wobbled, the tire flat. She got off. Oh, *please!* But yes. Flat, flat, *flat.* Ahead, maybe around the bend, was Healey's farm, maybe they'd have a bicycle pump. Not likely, but *maybe . . .*

The sound of a car behind her. "Ms Tunet!"

She turned her head. Blake Rossiter in a gray Lexus. "Trouble?" He smiled, his teeth very white beneath his sandy mustache. He wore a wine-colored turtleneck.

Five minutes later, for the second time in a week, Torrey's collapsible bike was put in the boot of a car. "No trouble at all," Blake Rossiter said, leaning over the boot and pushing aside an olive-green carton that, Torrey saw, was addressed to him care of his gallery on Aungier Street, in Dublin. "I'll go south on the access road to the village and drop you off at Duffy's Garage. Then I'm off to Dublin."

Beside him in the car, Torrey buckled her seat belt. "Thanks. Highly appreciated. Lucky you came along, *nobody* seems ever to use this back road." She was looking at his strong hands on the wheel. There was paint under his fingernails. "You've been out painting landscapes?"

"What? Right . . . right. Autumn colors in a Wicklow landscape." He ran a thumb and forefinger along his mustache and slanted a glance at her.

At Duffy's Garage, behind Nolan's Bed-and-Breakfast, Blake Rossiter said good-bye and watched Ms. Torrey Tunet wheel her bicycle over to young Billy Dugan. Then he turned the Lexus and headed for Dublin. Ms. Tunet. A kind of boyish elegance, even in jeans. Driving, he reached up and tipped the reflecting mirror down. He looked at his reflection. At his age, still handsome. His baldness didn't detract, what with the side-burns against his tanned skin. And with his lean figure, he didn't look sixty. Well, sixty-two.

Ms. Tunet. Intriguing thought. Slender, but naturally high-breasted, likely didn't even wear a . . . But . . . He frowned. Stay clear, stay clear, or before you knew it, she'd be dropping in at the lodge. He couldn't have that.

28

Monday, twelve noon, Michael McIntyre, at his table beside the window in O'Malley's Pub, ruffled his thicket of white hair, sipped from his pint and hopefully scanned the street through the window.

Three days of deprivation. Three days without even a glimpse of Ms. Torrey Tunet, thus depriving him of one of his daily pleasures. No jeans-clad Ms. Tunet, peacock bandanna around her wavy hair, skidding her bike to a stop and buying greens across the street at Coyle's or stopping next door at O'Curry's Meats for a chop or two, or, farther down Butler Street, going into Miss Amelia's Tea Shoppe for some ladylike sustenance. No Ms. Torrey Tunet, of the flower mouth and cool gray eyes starred by black lashes, dropping in to O'Malley's at lunchtime for the Daily Special and a chat.

"The Special," he said to Corinne, who appeared at his side. "And another pint."

But he knew Ms. Tunet was in Ballynagh. A jaunt last evening up the annex road, and through the hedge, and he'd glimpsed a light in the old groundsman's cottage. Was she all right? . . . Or perhaps lying sick and delirious within? He'd hesitated, then gone through the hedge and around the little pond and looked through the window beside the door, at the same time hearing an odd *slap, slap, slap* from within. And there she was, Ms. Torrey Tunet in jeans, at eleven o'clock at night, jumping rope, *slap, slap, slap* of rope on the floor, Ms. Tunet's brows drawn together in concentration. So she was all right. After a fashion.

Now, at noontime, McIntyre drained the pint, and over its rim saw, through O'Malley's window, Roger Flannery's new green Mercedes with its silver monogram glide by. The fellow was still back and forth between Gwathney Hall and Dublin. Spending his fortune. Buying an expensive house in Dublin. Boylston Street, in Ballsbridge. Hiring a decorator fellow. Flannery had got self-important. Had even — "The Special, Mr. McIntyre," Corinne set down the plate — had even last night at Finney's, having dinner with Blake Rossiter, the art-dealer fellow, been overheard giving Rossiter his opinion on the current market for artworks, and filling Rossiter in on the history of famous works of art. Rossiter, a handsome balding fellow in his sixties, with a peanut-colored mustache, had unconsciously clenched his fists on his knees, a fact that had been noted and reported to McIntyre himself by his old friend Dennis O'Curry of O'Curry's Meats: "It was like maybe Mrs. O'Brien telling me, for instance, how to cut pork for a crown roast! I'd crown *her!*"

McIntyre forked up the last mouthful of mashed potatoes. It was likely that Rossiter, the art-dealer fellow, suffered having dinner with Roger Flannery in hopes of selling him an expensive painting or two for that elegant house in Ballsbridge. Painful way of life, that must be, cozening up to —

"Dessert, Mr. McIntyre?" Corinne was at his elbow. "Today's is apple crisp."

McIntryre pulled his nose. "Guess not. I'm full up, Corinne." Waiting for his change, he spied across the street that pretty overweight Kathleen Hurley with Megan O'Faolain's little niece, both of them eating some sort of chocolate-looking bars.

Megan O'Faolain. McIntyre rumpled his thatch of hair. He knew who had stolen Jack McGuire's hog, knew which innocent-faced girl bedded a neighbor's husband, why this or that wife wept at night, and who hid gambling winnings under a board in his barn.

But as for Megan O'Faolain and Liam Caffrey, he knew only that Megan O'Faolain was sick in love with the man. He'd seen them walking together on the road below Castle Moore well over a month ago. He'd seen Megan turn her head and look up at Liam Caffrey walking beside her. And he, Michael McIntyre, who was seventy-six and had voyaged the world, and had strange and wonderful memories, had, for an instant, felt, sharp as a knife, a stab of envy.

29

At the kitchen table, the journal open before her, Torrey straightened, groaned, stretched and rubbed the back of her neck. The journal had the previous year's date on the first page, so John Gwathney had begun it in April, eighteen months ago. Black scratchings, a minuscule handwriting, sometimes digging into the page, other times gliding lightly as a swan on a lake.

Torrey rubbed her eyes. Exasperating that her poor knowledge of Greek made reading the journal that much more of a struggle.

Three days ago, that first afternoon, reading the journal and feeling guilty, she had stumbled on through the afternoon, hoping to find a clue that would point Inspector O'Hare's suspicions toward someone other than Megan O'Faolain. But those early pages had turned out to be John Gwathney's prosaic accounts of buying a plane ticket or going off by car or train to research old documents in musty archives. Disappointing. And next morning she was going to bring the journal to Inspector Egan O'Hare.

Yet, she had not. Because, next morning, at breakfast, opening the journal at random, she read in Greek: *Yes! Yes!* Exultant, Gwathney's pen digging deep. *Yes! Yes!* Followed by something illegible, and then, unexpectedly in English, *It was through the toothless beggar in front of the kiosk . . .*

A shiver slid down her spine. And she thought: No, Inspector O'Hare, not quite yet. She had glimpsed a tale that would surely become clear. Go back; go slowly.

She turned back the pages.

That second day, and through the evening and then until midnight, she had pored over the journal, feeling guilty and munching chocolate bars. Yet she'd managed to struggle through only a few more prosaic pages.

The morning of the third day, she put the journal in her shoulder bag, locked the cottage door, went out to the access road and flagged down the bus to Dublin. She returned at noon with a sackful of books that she dumped on the kitchen table: a Greek translation of Simenon's *Maigret and the Yellow Dog*, and a Greek grammar and dictionary. For a moment she stood looking down at the books. She had an odd feeling, like a fast heartbeat, or maybe it was something to do with the hasty pot-roast sandwich she'd had at a Bewley's; but she shivered. Anticipation? Apprehension? She could see Jasper's raised, questioning eyebrows, a little smile hovering around his mouth. He knew her too well.

In the late afternoon, when the phone rang, she didn't get up from the kitchen table where she sat with the journal, the Greek books, some scribbled notes of her own and a tepid mug of tea. From her answering machine she heard Myra Schwartz's voice from Boston: "Torrey! Why do you *have* e-mail if you never read it? Or are you out sheepherding or whatever you do in that bucolic corner of Eire? Portugal is on again, the embassy. Can you make it in three weeks? Are you, for God's sake, *there?* Hello to that Jasper of yours."

Absorbed, she barely heard. She lifted her head from the journal. She was hungry, she'd forgotten to have lunch, and anyway, she was almost out of food; she should stock up in the village. Maybe later.

The phone rang again. Carefully she put the sugar bowl on the journal page to hold her place, and crossed to the desk. "Hello?"

"My love, you sound twenty leagues under the sea. Surface. Tell me all."

"Jasper, I have John Gwathney's journal." She told him about finding the journal in Roger Flannery's rooms, and then about the drugs. "So that must be where Flannery's salary was going."

"Right. Up his nose or into his arm. Could've been costing him plenty. More than he had? Drug dealers at his heels? In any case, lucky for Flannery that he inherited the

Landseer. But his stealing Gwathney's journal from the cottage . . . Why? Maybe afraid the journal would reveal his addiction."

"I left the drugs. I only took the journal. Of course I'll give it to Inspector O'Hare. But I'm sort of dipping into it. Just to take a look. I was hoping, I'm *still* hoping to find a lead that will clear Megan O'Faolain. Inspector O'Hare is up on his hind legs, sniffing the air, determined to indict her and Liam Caffrey for Gwathney's —"

"And you've found?"

"So far, nothing to help Megan. The journal's early part, which is as far as I've got, seems to be about John Gwathney's research, that book he maybe burned. He seems to be searching for something, I don't yet know what. Involves Irish history, something about Baltimore, in Cork."

"*West* Cork. Baltimore, on the harbor, is down in that wild sea area, all touristed up now. Not far from Kinsale, the best gourmet food in Ireland. Crabs in a butter sauce with just a hint of —"

"*Aside* from the crabs."

"Old history. Infamous. *The Sack of Baltimore*. In the mid–sixteen hundreds, around sixteen-thirty, Algerian pirates landed and raided Baltimore, massacred some inhabitants and captured over a hundred people and took them away as slaves to North Africa.

Children and all. God help them. Torrey? You there?"

"Barely." The phone was slippery, her hand was wet.

"Barbary pirates. The seas were teeming with them. Algiers, Morocco, Tunis, Tripoli. Kidnapping along the coasts. If you were lucky, you might be ransomed. That seldom happened."

Torrey took a deep breath. She looked over at John Gwathney's journal on the kitchen table, the sugar bowl holding down her page.

"Torrey? You're on my mind," Jasper said. "But when are you not? I called to tell you that eight days from now you may find me on your doorstep with a heart full of devotion and a recipe for crab-and-shrimp torte. If I'm lucky, you won't have been co-opted by Interpreters International. Or . . ." He paused. "By anything else."

30

It was frightening; Kathleen had never seen Roger Flannery like that — his face so white and his eyes furious. The little ponytail at his nape had got loose and a thin lock of hair hung down over the collar of his cashmere jacket. He stood in the doorway of Sharon's room, where Kathleen and Sharon had been looking at a kids' television show about ballet. Ms. O'Faolain was out, and Mr. Flannery still had a key to Gwathney Hall, what with not having yet wholly moved out. Minutes ago, she'd glimpsed him passing Sharon's room, then heard him going up the stairs to the third floor. Now here he was, five minutes later, standing in the doorway of Sharon's room, looking so awful and breathing fast. *"When?"* Mr. Flannery said again.

"Last week," Kathleen said. "I had to go to my weight-loss group in the village. And Ms. O'Faolain had to go off to the lawyers in Dublin. So Ms. Tunet said she'd take care of Sharon until I got back. So . . . Well, that's all."

Mr. Flannery nodded. Then he went calm. He smoothed back his loosened hair and clipped it at his nape with the little silver clip. He turned and went downstairs.

In the Pearse Street flat, at eight o'clock, he stood by the window, fists clenched, gazing blankly out into the dark street. Ms. Torrey Tunet. She'd been in his rooms at Gwathney Hall and stolen the journal. John Gwathney's journal was the only thing that had stood in his way. What the journal would tell . . .

Ironic. The journal. He'd had it, he'd *had* it, he'd meant finally to destroy it, but stupidly . . . But at least she'd overlooked the drugs. A fortune's worth, those three little packets.

"Roger?" He turned around. Cherry, slender, in high heels, black satin pants and a violet-colored silk shirt, positioned herself squarely in front of him, her pert face serious. "Now. Do you like it better *with* the flower" — she held the rose-shaped diamond pin to the shoulder of her shirt — "or without?" She whisked the diamond pin away.

"With." He'd bought the rose pin yesterday at Weir's on Grafton Street.

"Me, too."

It was almost eight o'clock, they should be off, Cherry wanted to go to that club on Wellington Quay where Paul McCartney, *Sir* Paul McCartney, had appeared last year.

142

Cherry was up on all that. A whole world out there, while he'd been buried in old books and libraries. Trapped. But at least there'd been Cherry, falling asleep in the worn armchair those evenings she could get away from that bastard and come to him. Now all their evenings would be together. "I'm taking just a lipstick and my comb," Cherry said.

"Right." He smiled at Cherry, but he was seeing John Gwathney's limp pocket journal. Ironic that, after everything, John Gwathney had left him a valuable painting.

31

At nine-thirty on a rainy afternoon, Torrey went through the Nassau Street entrance to Trinity College. She kept one hand on her shoulder bag, which held her wallet, a couple of chocolate bars, a lipstick, a pen, a pad and John Gwathney's journal. She had wrapped the journal in an outsized plastic sandwich bag to protect it. The journal's pages were thin, the jagged handwriting was tiny, and John Gwathney had written on both sides of the pages, making the writing more difficult to read because the words on one side often blotted through to the other side. Torrey had had a headache for almost a week now.

At the entrance to the Old Library, she paid the one-pound fifty shillings, then hesitated, looking about. Here in these rooms, which were already filling up with tourists, was Ireland's finest collection of Greek, Egyptian, Latin and Irish manuscripts.

"Ms. Tunet?" A short, balding man with a jolly-looking face was at her elbow. "I'm Joseph Flynn. Mr. Shaw described you quite . . . quite adequately." He blushed.

Thank you, Mr. Jasper Shaw. Was there anyone Jasper *didn't* know? She followed Mr.

Flynn down a corridor in this Ancient Manuscript Section of the Library of the University of Dublin.

A small, quiet room with a pneumatic door that hissed closed. Two women staff members looked up from their desks, smiled, then looked down again at their work.

"Over here." A table and chair; on the table were three books and several documents in celluloid envelopes. "No smoking, of course," Joseph Flynn said; and he left her.

. . . *rampaged along the coasts of Spain, England, and other European and Mediterranean countries, taking captives. Every member of a Barbary pirate ship's crew received a portion of the proceeds of the valuable cargo of captives.*

. . . *have learned that on landing in Algiers, the captives are taken to the* zoco, *the slave market, where the* dey *makes his choice first. The rest are bartered or sold to the highest bidder. The children are separated from their parents and sold as household slaves.*

That was the fate of the one hundred men, women, and children kidnapped from Baltimore. The possibility of ransom was near non-existent, and no ransom is known of.

A church tower bonged the noon hour. One of the women staff members put on her coat and left; the door hissed closed behind her. Torrey, dazed, looked up from the document.

"Lunchtime." The remaining staff member got up. "Sorry, but I can't leave you alone here."

"That's all right." Torrey slipped the document back into its celluloid cover.

32

At eight o'clock on a windy morning, Inspector Egan O'Hare drove the police car up the rutted road and stopped behind the giant digger that said SULLIVAN & SONS on its side. The digger, rumbling, was clawing up great gobs of stony earth. Its driver, in a billed cap, waved down at the police car.

An instant later, the digger's rumble stopped and Brian Sullivan climbed down. "Damned cell phone. All I got was that you were coming." He waved at his two sons, who were leaning on their shovels and watching, and they went back to shoveling.

"So . . . ?" Brian, a hulk of a man, resettled his cap and took out a crushed pack of cigarettes.

"The Caffrey job," O'Hare said, "that pottery shop. Two years or so ago, wasn't it?"

"That's right. Cigarette? No? Roof, interior work, new window frames. Turned out there was no cellar and the floors had been rotting. Then electricity had to be boosted; Caffrey wanted two kilns for the pottery. Had to call in a special guy from Athy. Besides that, the fireplace chimney needed more than pointing, too many bricks gone. Major stuff, all around." He lit a cigarette, shielding the match from the wind. "Turned out to be a bigger job than Liam Caffrey had expected. City man. Fell into an expensive pile of . . . manure."

"So . . . You had a contract?" And at Brian Sullivan's nod: "Any trouble Caffrey paying?"

Brian Sullivan said, "Well, now." He looked quizzically back at Inspector O'Hare. "The contract was . . . The deal was in thirds. First payment was right on the nose. The second payment . . ." Sullivan shrugged. "Lagged by a couple of months, but then he promised it right away, and four months later his check came through. Didn't like to lean on the fellow, this is Ballynagh, not Dublin or Galway. Besides, I figured, the man's an artist, you know artists. Impractical."

"Yes," O'Hare said. "Right. Impractical. And the third payment?"

Brian Sullivan flipped his cigarette into the muddy maw at their feet. "I can guess why you're asking, Egan. I know what they're saying in the village." He gnawed at his lip. "He put it off, and off. Promising. Then, two months ago, he said it was only a matter of weeks; he had funds coming in."

A gust of wind blew a dead branch against Brian Sullivan's boot. He picked it up and tossed it away. "Two weeks ago, he paid. A check for four thousand pounds."

O'Hare drove back up the rutted road. Behind him, he heard the rumble of the digger starting up.

Two weeks ago. Time for Megan O'Faolain to have withdrawn cash from her inheritance of the John Gwathney estate. Still, only supposition. Not as though he had located, for instance, the murder weapon. The shotgun. Where was it? He had no clue. As yet. *As yet.*

By nine o'clock, he was back in the police station, where Sergeant Jimmy Bryson greeted him with the news that Rosaleen O'Shea, who every other week did the laundry at Gwathney Hall, would arrive at ten o'clock in answer to Inspector O'Hare's telephoned message to her mother's house.

"A Tuesday, I always did Gwathney Hall on the alternate Tuesdays. It was the end of September. Mr. Gwathney was away, off on one of his trips to a foreign country, like he does. And . . . I don't like to gossip, but this isn't gossip, it's part of an investigation, after all. So that makes it all right. Otherwise, I wouldn't *dream* . . ."

Inspector O'Hare, regarding Rosaleen O'Shea, who sat across from his desk, put up a hand and covered his smile. Rosaleen O'Shea, aged only twenty-two, was doubtless headed for a career as a gossip columnist on one of those scandal sheets in Dublin. A bee spreading pollen, Rosaleen O'Shea was a brown-haired girl with a sharp little nose, light blue eyes that saw everything, and normal-sized ears that heard every rumor in its embryonic state and built thereon. Inquisitive as all get-out. Always on the phone to Hannah, Sergeant Jimmy Bryson's girlfriend, because what good was finding out something if you couldn't pass it on? That's what made it so delicious. Not to mention knowing it *first*. Rosaleen O'Shea and Hannah had been friends since about the age of seven and had the special bond of being born on exactly the same day. So Hannah always got the news first. Hannah, feeling she ought not to let the news go to waste, always passed it along to Jimmy Bryson, who in this case had alerted Inspector O'Hare. "Might be something there?"

"Might be." So here was Rosaleen O'Shea in fleece jacket, calf-length checked skirt and boots. And with something ugly she'd told Hannah about. In the chair across from O'Hare's desk, she leaned forward.

"Ms. O'Faolain had been out all afternoon. I knew she was at the pottery shop, that's where she'd go, to be with *him*. It was a chilly day, damp and miserable. When she got back to the Hall, she was shivering and wanted a hot bath. I'd just finished a batch of towels, they were still warm from the drier, so I brought one to her room. She was just coming from her bath. She was naked. There was a shockingly ugly bruise on her breast. She tried to hide it, but I saw. I wouldn't be telling you, Inspector, except . . . you know. As part of the investigation. Besides, I feel sorry for Megan O'Faolain. You can almost tell, just by looking at his face — dark, like a gypsy's."

On the way out, Rosaleen O'Shea wiggled her fingers good-bye to Sergeant Jimmy Bryson.

33

The moon shone down on the rhododendrons that grew thick along the front of Gwathney Hall, turning the evergreen leaves to silver. The two massive iron lamps beside the double front doors gleamed yellow. It was eight o'clock, a dry, chilly evening.

At eight o'clock exactly, Kathleen, who was helping out tonight, stood at the top of the broad steps, ready to let in the four dinner guests.

There was no door to the drawing room where the terrible murder of John Gwathney had happened, just the wide entrance off the hall. So Ms. O'Faolain had had a green velvet rope drawn across the entrance to the drawing room and the before-dinner drinks were to be served in the sitting room on the opposite side of the hall. Kathleen was to direct the guests.

The first to arrive was Mr. Liam Caffrey. He had come the half mile from the pottery shop on foot. Letting him in, Kathleen blushed in embarrassment because of the gossip about him and Ms. O'Faolain, but she couldn't help it. He wasn't in his usual black turtleneck, but wore a smoky-looking jacket over an open-throated white shirt. Not hand-some. Just this side of ugly, in an attractive way that gave you a bit of a shiver. His dark hair, thick and curly, was close-cropped. He was dark-browed with flat cheeks and a jut-ting mouth. There was a curved little line on each side of his mouth, so that at first look you'd think he was smiling, but then it was as though he'd just said something sarcastic, although he hadn't. It was sexy, somehow.

Ms. Tunet arrived on her bicycle, wearing high-heeled silver shoes, and with a soft-looking green dress all gathered up high over her knees away from the pedals. She was fol-lowed by Ms. Winifred Moore, who zoomed up in her red Jeep. Ms. Moore, in Kathleen's opinion, was a hazard on the road, jolting madly along, especially when she was wearing her dashing Australian outback hat; it made her extra reckless.

Mr. Blake Rossiter came last, in a sleek gray Lexus. In Kathleen's opinion, and as she said to her older sister Norah in the kitchen, Ms. O'Faolain felt obliged to invite Mr. Rossiter because he'd called her so many times, offering to drive her to Dublin to fancy art gallery shows that served wine and tiny sandwiches, and last week sending around a box of various jams from all over the world, a dozen jars packed in straw. Kathleen understood, from overhearing a thing or two, that Mr. Rossiter would get a commission — "*Thousands* of pounds, maybe!" — if Megan O'Faolain, in deciding to sell Gwathney Hall and its furnishings, sold the remaining two or three paintings through him. "That's what Mr. Rossiter is angling for, sending Ms. O'Faolain flowers and foreign fruit and all," Kathleen had told her sister Norah. "Now that she's so rich, people are after her for all kinds of things. Some folks want her to donate money to help unmarried teenage mothers. The mail she gets! Other folks wanting her to buy fancy linens, underwear, or to rent a villa in the south of France. Like that. Honestly! It's positively frightening!"

"That's the usual," Norah had nodded. Norah cooked out for dinner parties and was sophisticated.

It was Norah in the kitchen tonight, doing the cooking. Ms. O'Faolain would've got Mary O'Brien to do the serving, but Sharon had the sniffles and was in bed, so she'd asked Kathleen. Extra pay. Kathleen wore a blue dress with a starched white apron and black stockings and shoes.

A chill wind blew, and Kathleen, shivering, closed the great front doors. She started across the hall toward the sitting room, where she'd be helping serve the drinks, when she heard a noise behind her from the drawing room. Something. A rustle, like someone moving. She turned and looked and saw that the green velvet rope across the entrance to the drawing room was still in place. She hesitated, then went slowly toward the drawing room and looked across the velvet rope into the room, which was kept softly lit by the rose-shaded lamp on the grand piano.

A figure on the rug by the piano. "Mr. Rossiter!"

He was kneeling on one knee, scanning beneath the piano. At her exclamation, he stood up and straightened his jacket. His face was flushed. "Kathleen, isn't it? Startled you, did I? I'm playing detective. I don't trust the Gardaí's proficiency in examining a crime scene. They always miss something. It helps to have an artist's eye." And Mr. Rossiter tapped the outer corner of his right eye. "So I said to myself: Have a look around. Maybe you can turn up something the Gardaí overlooked. It's the least I could do to help Ms. O'Faolain." He slapped a hand across the knees of his trousers.

"The Gardaí brought a vacuum cleaner from Dublin Castle," Kathleen said.

"Of course, of course!" Mr. Rossiter said, sounding impatient. "But that doesn't necessarily . . . Ah, well . . . Drinks in the sitting room, is it?"

'Yes, sir." She followed him across the hall.

In the sitting room, Kathleen belatedly helped serve the before-dinner drinks. Ms.

O'Faolain sipped sherry. She was quiet and looked beautiful, her dark hair sleeked back and her eyes so startlingly blue. She wore a loosely knitted coral-colored silk top with wide sleeves like trumpets. The way she looked at Liam Caffrey . . . "Well, it's plain she'd do anything for him," Kathleen said later to Norah.

Liam Caffrey had a whiskey. Winifred Moore had a vodka neat, then signaled Kathleen for another and tossed it down. "God knows how the Russians discovered heaven in a potato," Winifred Moore said, grinning. Her friend, Sheila Flaxton, wasn't there; she was in London "to put the magazine to bed," Winifred Moore said. Blake Rossiter had something pale green called an aperitif.

As for Ms. Torrey Tunet, she said, "What? Oh, well, can I make myself a martini?" And she did, which was a good thing, because Kathleen had no idea how to. Ms. Tunet was pale and hollow-eyed. Her gray eyes starred by the short black lashes looked tired. A silky swath of hair fell across her forehead. She had on a warm-looking green velour dress and dangling gold earrings and looked so-phisticated, as she must look going around Europe and interpreting, instead of riding her bike around Ballynagh in jeans and a jumper. She hadn't much to say; and at dinner she ate automatically, "like someone hypnotized," Kathleen told Norah. Still, Ms. Tunet man-

156

aged to eat heartily of the ham and even had two helpings of the dessert, which was chocolate mousse.

Kathleen wondered why Ms. O'Faolain was giving this dinner party. Maybe it was because Ms. Winifred Moore was the social arbiter of Ballynagh? Not that Winifred Moore cared two pins about *being* a social arbiter. But for over three hundred years, the village had looked to Castle Moore when there had been a drought, a political skirmish, a warring over land boundaries. And now, there had been a murder.

So Megan O'Faolain had seated Winifred Moore next to Liam Caffrey. They were getting on remarkably, discussing something called *raku* and talking about hand-thrown pottery and matte and crackle glazes.

It was sad that Ms. O'Faolain might think there was any way for Ballynagh to accept Liam Caffrey, Winifred Moore or not, when everybody in the village knew that through the investigative abilities of Inspector Egan O'Hare, it could well be revealed that . . . Kathleen looked at the dark-browed Liam Caffrey and felt a coldness so that she rubbed her arms.

"Grecian pottery," Winifred Moore was saying to Mr. Liam Caffrey. "The figures of Grecian nymphs on black pottery, exquisite work." She went on about Grecian women and their status in ancient Greece, and then she turned to Ms. Tunet and said, "Didn't I see you in Waterstone's in Dublin? Buying a Greek dictionary? I was in a rush or I would've . . . But I thought you were heading for *Portugal*. Or not?"

"In Waterstone's?" And then Ms. Tunet jerked her hand and her wineglass tipped over, and she never did get to say about Portugal. She yawned a lot and left early.

34

Friday morning, in the breakfast room at Castle Moore, Winifred swallowed the last bite of muffin, licked a bit of butter off her thumb and said, "If you ask *me*, Sheila, there was no need to exhaust yourself in London, you have a staff there for —"

"A *staff*? Two people, Winifred! And Eugene Willey is eighty-two years old! I can't exactly trust —"

"You missed Megan O'Faolain's dinner party. Lovely, but what with the drawing room roped off, it only makes one imagine even more, the gruesome —"

"*Please*, Winifred!"

"Really, Sheila, don't be so . . . Anyway, I had a fascinating conversation with Liam Caffrey, the presumed murderer of —"

"Winifred! For heaven's sake! How can you be so —"

"— and found Mr. Caffrey totally fascinating about women in the arts in ancient Rome and Greece. Women *artisans!* While universities load only classical studies about Platos and their ilk onto their students. No mention! — None! — of women who actually took clay into their hands! I've already started a group of sonnets on the subject."

"Sonnets? If you can manage three, for the spring issue, Winifred, that would be —"

"Of course I can." Winifred drained her teacup. "Anyway, yesterday afternoon I stopped by Gwathney Hall to bring Megan some plantings I'd promised her. Roger Flannery was there in the drive, moving his things out, piling them into that beautiful monster of a car. Wearing well-tailored city clothes, cuff links and all."

"Well, why *not?* He certainly deserves —"

"Day before yesterday, I was in Dublin and was passing Weir's on Grafton Street. I stopped in to have a look at their fabulous jewelry, I never can resist, though I wouldn't spend one shilling . . . Anyway, there, shopping at a counter of truly glittering necklaces, diamonds, and I think emeralds, was Roger Flannery with a young woman in a beret. She had red hair and a pointed chin and green eyes. The clerk had just finished wrapping their package and was bowing all over himself, handing it to them. When they went out, I saw the young woman had a limp. A pity. I think Roger saw me. Anyway, he whisked the girl into his car and off they went."

"I do think it's nice" — Sheila cut a muffin in half — "for Roger to be rich now, and to have a girl. And maybe marry."

But Winifred was frowning. "Something

about Roger Flannery . . . something. Always had an air of . . . As though he thought he'd been done dirt. Why, I can't guess. John Gwathney was wonderful to him. Once told me about it, his finding Roger as a lad. John turned him from a grub into a gent. Though I abhor that ponytail."

35

In Algiers, it took me some days to locate the old library. There is little French spoken since the departure of the French, and almost no English, and I knew none of the Berber dialects. But thanks to my years of research in the Near East, my Arabic, though far from fluent, carried me through. And at last I found my way.

The library was in a decrepit state. But there, after exhaustively poring over tattered pages, I found listings of sales of captives kidnapped from Spain and other coasts. And finally, among them, I found mention of a sale of captives from Ireland in the year 1631.

It was in that listing of the sale of captives from Baltimore, Ireland, that I came across this sentence that changed everything for me: One child was deemed less valuable, having only four fingers of the right hand, the little finger missing, so was bought at a cheaper price by a Berber sect which also acquired several other children as slaves.

Torrey, sitting crouched over at the kitchen table, felt a strange excitement. For five hours she had sat there, translating the journal and transcribing the sentences in a loose-leaf eight-by-ten notebook. She was hungry, starved. It was getting on to three o'clock and her eyes felt grainy. But impossible to stop now! She read on, transcribing, until she had the next paragraph:

"A child deemed less valuable." With the strangest feeling, I recalled my exhaustive historical research of the kidnapped Baltimore families, among them Celia and Desmond Creedon and their six-year-old child, Annabel, and of the genetic fault in the Creedons: the missing last finger.

Torrey sat back, her heart beating fast. She unwrapped the silver paper from a chocolate bar, bit into it, and after a full five minutes went back to the laborious translation. A half hour later she had the next paragraph transcribed. She read it aloud in a whisper:

At once my projected book disappeared and another arose, irresistibly, in its place. I could only think: That child! That child! I am not insane, it is possible.

She could not stop now. John Gwathney's handwriting in the next paragraph was more erratic, more difficult to read. But finally she had that last short paragraph on the page:

This sect, Berbers from the west of Tripoli, left before nightfall with their new slaves, returning to that desert country, to their religious, fortress-like enclosure.

Torrey's hand trembled on the Greek dictionary. She looked up. A religious enclosure? In contemporary parlance . . . a monastery?

36

In O'Malley's Pub, a few minutes to six
o'clock on Friday night, young Jack O'Malley,
tending bar, finished cutting up the cubes of
cheese. He stuck toothpicks in the cubes and
piled them into three dishes and set them at
intervals along the bar. The big television
screen overhead behind him was already on.
In the last few minutes the bar had become
crowded. No one wanted to miss Mickey
O'Boyle's *Inquiry*.

Mickey O'Boyle, the highly paid television
commentator, was the size of a jockey and
had a mouth that stretched widely toward his
ears. In a staccato delivery, he zeroed in on
cheating supermarkets, dangerous fat-
reducing drugs, a dirty-mouthed guitar singer
and politicians on the take. You could count
on Mickey O'Boyle not to let the liars,
cheaters or murderers slip by undetected.
Friday night with Mickey O'Boyle's *Inquiry*
was not to be missed.

But this Friday, what a shock! The crowd
at the bar at O'Malley's went dead quiet.

"Ballynagh," Mickey O'Boyle said, first
thing out of the box, "a village in Wicklow,
where dwelled John Gwathney, one of Ire-

land's foremost historians. Murdered with a shotgun. Blasted off the face of the earth. Yet weeks have gone by with no sign of progress in the investigation. Too much for the local Gardaí in Ballynagh? But the village of Ballynagh is in the Dublin metropolitan area, which, for some doubtless brilliant reason, includes portions of counties Kildare and Wicklow. So where is Dublin Castle in this affair? Is the Gwathney murder inquiry as dead as the famous historian? How about some answers, Dublin Castle? The public deserves even a lack-of-progress report."

"My!" Cherry looked at Roger Flannery with big questioning eyes. Lying on the sofa before the television set with her bare feet across Roger's lap, she wore a cozy white chenille robe with a shawl collar, from which Roger had clipped the price tag barely an hour ago. Roger was in his maroon robe, having just showered. Soon, they'd dress and be off to dinner. Later they'd drop in at another new club on Harcourt Street that Cherry knew about.

"D'you *think*," Cherry went on, "that the woman who inherited Gwathney Hall . . . what's her name?"

"Megan O'Faolain."

"D'you think *she* might've had something to do with it? The murder?"

"God knows." He chafed one of Cherry's

bare feet between his hands. "Your toes are cold, it's this flat, no fire can warm it. Thank God that three months from now we'll be in our own house in Ballsbridge."

"And live happily ever after," Cherry said. She smiled at him, and he smiled back.

In the sitting room at Castle Creedon, Willow, cross-legged on the rug before the television set, said, "Wow! That Mickey O'Boyle! Keeps the sluggish blood boiling!" She looked at Buddy, her twin, lying on his stomach on the rug beside her, then at her parents. "Gwathney. That's the old guy who visited us. The fellow who's crackers, right?"

"For sure," Buddy said, "the guy who swiped that crummy old hairbrush. Right, Ma?"

Constance Thorpe didn't even look up from her knitting. "I guess so." She was in the club chair by the fire, working on the left sleeve of the sweater, right at the shoulder, which required all her attention. But for an instant, her glance went to her husband. Owen was standing beside the fire, the bowl of his pipe cupped in his hand. He frowned at Buddy. "This fellow, Mickey O'Boyle. He's a damned alarmist! Of course the Gardaí is competently investigating the Gwathney murder! Of course! *Damn!*" His pipe had fallen from his hand. It clattered against the grate.

37

"I'm hungry as a horse, Sheila, but first, our business with Blake Rossiter. *Then,* Finney's."

Winifred drove the red Jeep with careless ease. She wore her outback hat and an old plaid muffler slung around her neck over her oatmeal sweater. The wind blew across the road, rattling the loose windshield. It was almost noon. "I am *not,* after all, a rich woman, Sheila, not to mention the horrendous taxes on Castle Moore. So, Blake Rossiter."

Sheila, huddling beside her, wearing her knitted Yugoslavian woolen cap and an array of heavy scarves, said, "But *Sisters in Poetry* is perfectly —"

"You delude yourself, Sheila. You need a bigger staff in London, preferably a female under the age of eighty. And I'm hoping that at least *one* of those dusty old paintings that I inherited from my asinine, odious, *loathsome* cousin Desmond, along with Castle Moore, just *might* be worth —" She swerved, then slowed the Jeep. "It's that road on the right, up through those woods. Blake Rossiter's weekend 'retreat,' as he calls it." She looked at the clock on the dashboard. "I told him twelve noon. We're exactly on time."

The room smelled of leather and whiskey. "Belonged to the Fitzgerald family; I've had it ten years now." Blake Rossiter, handsome in a comfortable-looking coat sweater, poured hot tea from a glass carafe and handed the cup to Sheila, who, settled on a soft brown suede chair, gratefully closed her icy fingers around the cup.

Winifred, standing by the broad fireplace that held a crackling fire, looked appraisingly about. Oak-beamed ceiling, mahogany mantel that held a row of beautifully carved duck decoys. Brown suede couch and fat brown suede chairs. On the walls, landscape watercolors. In an alcove to the left, she glimpsed hunting and fishing gear. Above was a balcony with a lush thick-looking Kurdish rug hanging over the polished mahogany railing. The room was as handsome as Blake Rossiter.

"Admirable," Winifred said. She took the cup of tea he handed her. "No need to waste time. What I want, Blake . . . Megan O'Faolain tells me you offered to handle the sale of the two or three paintings at Gwathney Hall. If she decides to sell the Hall."

Blake Rossiter nodded. "Definitely. That's my business. Dealing in fine paintings."

"Well, then! I inherited Castle Moore four

years ago, but what with being in London most of the year, and my poetry, I haven't . . . There are a few musty miles of Castle Moore's corridors and bedrooms, and lately I'm thinking that surely, among all the carved old bedsteads and antiques and tapestries, there might be at least *one* painting about which you might be able to say, *Eureka!* And for which you could get me a good price."

Blake Rossiter, smiling, said, "Be glad to take a look." He glanced over at Sheila, whose chilled fingers still warmed themselves around the cup. "More tea?"

But Sheila, holding the empty teacup on her knee, only bit her lip and looked despairingly over at Winifred, who said reproachfully, "Oh, really, Sheila! You always . . . I *told* you, before we left . . ." And to Blake Rossiter: "The bathroom, if you don't mind."

Ten minutes later, having arranged a day next week for Blake Rossiter's visit to Castle Moore, they were off, the Jeep rattling down the road.

"What happened?" Winifred said. "When you and Blake came back, after he went looking for you, he looked so . . . so exasperated."

Sheila sighed. "When I left the bathroom I made a wrong turn and came into a workroom. Canvases stacked! Works in progress, landscapes. I know Blake is a Sunday painter, so . . . Anyway, I heard him behind me. 'Looking at my dabblings?' he said. He sounded amused. But I'd invaded his privacy. He was exasperated. I could tell."

"Next time, go to the bathroom *before* we go off on a jaunt," Winifred said. "I do hope Blake will find at least one worthwhile painting at Castle Moore. Just *one* would pay for staffing a half dozen *Sisters in Poetry* offices."

"And maybe even enough," Sheila said tartly, "to have Duffy's Garage fix that rattling windshield about which I *admittedly* have been nagging you for weeks now."

38

"Emmet," Sharon said, and she put her hands on her hips and looked up at her Auntie Megan. "If you ask *me*, that's a dumb name. *I* would've named him George. George is my favorite name."

Megan suddenly knelt and put her arms around Sharon and rocked her back and forth, her face in Sharon's neck. "You are the *dearest* . . ." She drew back and smiled at Sharon. "I'll miss you. But so does your mother. She can hardly wait to see you. She wants to introduce you to Emmet. He's now eight weeks old. With blue eyes." They were in Sharon's room. It was close to Christmas. Sharon was already packed. Besides the tan canvas tote bag she'd brought with her to Gwathney Hall all those weeks ago, she now had a real suitcase on wheels like Ms. Tunet's. Auntie Megan had helped her to pack it. It had her new clothes and the play makeup and two books and the embroidered guest towel for her mother. She and Kathleen had each embroidered a guest towel from the Grogan Sisters Knitting Shop. Kathleen's was for her sister. Sharon would go on the bus to Dublin. Her brother Henry, who was sixteen, would meet her at the bus stop.

They went downstairs. Auntie Megan wore boots and her long red woolen skirt and the gray jacket with the cozy high collar, but no hat. The damp weather had made her dark hair curly, all around her forehead and ears.

They were barely downstairs when they heard the bell, and the door opened and there was Mr. Blake Rossiter in a duffel coat and a cap with earflaps. He was carrying a shopping bag. "Cold as the devil outside! My vintner sent me six bottles of this special Rothschild and I thought, Why not give a couple of bottles to Ms. O'Faolain? Very special, this Rothschild vintage. With my compliments." And he stroked the sides of his mustache.

Auntie Megan thanked Mr. Rossiter. What surprised Sharon was that her Auntie Megan sounded like a mechanical doll when she talked with Mr. Blake Rossiter, which was often, because Mr. Blake Rossiter turned up often. He talked a lot about "poor John," whom Sharon didn't know, and as though they'd been close friends, he and "poor John," but it seemed that it only annoyed Auntie Megan, who was polite and smiled, but Sharon could tell. Her mother had that same look when she wanted to bash one of the kids but didn't.

Megan drove the Rover up the west road.

She had put Sharon on the bus to Dublin and paid Kathleen, the nanny, and then dropped her off in the village. She felt unutterably alone. Soon she would be selling Gwathney Hall. She would tell Liam that she agreed. They would go away, he'd talked of the southwest, not a city, but somewhere in the countryside.

She drove slowly, the sun shone. Here on the west road that led to the pottery shop and, beyond, to Gwathney Hall, there were no hedges and fields. This side of Ballynagh was forested with oak and elm and spruce. The road wound through the woods, briers on either side. The sunlight made patterns on the leaves, patterns that would be lovely, woven as scarves, throws, luxurious curtains. Once she had been a weaver like her father, weaving checked and striped and dappled woolens . . .

Once she had had a husband named Gahan O'Faolain, who had been studying to be an engineer until the cruel landslide in Drumcliff left him with a spinal injury, helpless in a wheelchair, unable even to guide a pencil. He'd been twenty-four.

After that, she had cared only to make Gahan laugh, which was like climbing a mountain every day, because how could there be much for Gahan to laugh about? So in their three-room flat in Athlone, she wove the striped and checked and dappled woolens and sold them in the front room.

"He didn't ask me to help him die," she'd told John Gwathney in that wonderful first year at Gwathney Hall, when she confided so much to him. "I'm sure it was for me that he hung on, year after year, until . . ."

Until that day when a young couple arrived at the flat with their little girl, a two-year-old, and while they were discussing which pattern of curtains to be woven, the child had picked up a pair of scissors and wandered into the bedroom where Gahan in his wheelchair sat staring at television. "How he got the scissors from the child, we never knew . . . or that he had the strength to bring it to his throat . . ." And she added, "He did it to free me. I'm sure of it." She was by then thirty-six. A year later she arrived in Ballynagh, a weaver with a dozen new sketched designs and the little she possessed.

Now, on the west road, on a rise on the left, she glimpsed Castle Moore with its north tower dating from the sixteen hundreds. Ivy covered the gray stone walls. So now it was only a half mile to the pottery shop.

"Liam?" She stood just inside the door of the shop and looked about. Where was he? Sunlight poured through the wide front windows. It shone on the shelves and tables of pottery, some pieces delicate as glass, others squat and solid, some glazed, or with finishes that had once been unknown to her.

"Christ! Good thing it's you!" He stood in the narrow doorway that led to the living quarters. He wore a faded East Indian robe and was toweling his dark hair dry. "I forgot to lock the door and put out the 'Closed' sign." He went past her, locked the door, and hung up the sign. When he turned back, his dark-browed face was unsmiling, and the curved little line on each side of his mouth was deep. "I had a call from a friend in Galway. My former marriage is being investigated. Inspector O'Hare, of course. Foraging."

"But . . ." She felt sick, her heart beat fast, she put a hand to her breast as though to still it. They would revive that scandal that was in his past. There would be photographs of the two women. As for the present . . . She looked away. She knew very well about the gossip in Ballynagh. She and Liam, her betrayal of John Gwathney. It had got about. And, uglier, like a shadow following her, that unspoken suspicion. Shopping at O'Curry's Meats, she couldn't help but see the way Dennis O'Curry's eyes slid aside and his face reddened as he handed her the package in the shiny paper across the counter; or how, at Coyle's, buying greens . . . But never mind. Never mind the ache in her heart. She would follow wherever Liam Caffrey led.

"It's chilly in here," she said. Yet she shrugged out of her gray jacket with the high collar.

39

The Berber at the wheel of this ancient Ford chants under his breath and bites into chunks of bread and hoists a water bottle to his lips. His name is Chadli and he is perhaps twenty, and bearded.

I am feverish with elation. For three days we have been traveling south. In Algiers I found Chadli through El Massaa, *the Arabic-language daily. He belongs to one of the Tuareg-speaking tribes in the south of the country, where they speak Berber dialects. He is delighted that his cousin, who cleans toilets at* El Massaa, *provided him with a well-paying passenger home. I would have paid a fortune to travel south through this rugged range of mountains. They sweep from Morocco on the west to Tunisia on the east and are laced with roads.*

Wednesday . . . *At last, the desert. Blinding sun, desert roads, gravel at first, then of sand. Like mirages, dusty villages appear. Almost no Arabic is spoken here in these busy streets. Kabyle is the language, or Tuareg. Flies, spices; my skin burns . . .*

Torrey looked up from the journal's stained

pages. She stretched her fingers, which were cramped from transcribing the Greek translation into her loose-leaf notebook. The cottage had gotten chilly, she should put more peat on the fire. It was already four o'clock, wind rattled the windows, a branch made a scraping sound against the window over the kitchen sink. These last three days, it seemed always to have become four o'clock and dusk whenever she looked up from the journal.

"Enough!" she said aloud. She closed the Greek dictionary and pushed away the journal. She got up, stretched widely, groaned and took her jump rope from the hook beside the door. Holding the rope, she stood a moment, bemused, gazing into space. *Flies, spices; my skin burns.* She blinked, shrugged, hung the jump rope back on the hook, sat down again at the kitchen table, opened the journal, pulled her loose-leaf notebook closer and again picked up her pencil.

She didn't hear the clock strike five, didn't hear it strike six.

Sunday . . . *Maziba is the old man's name. Maziba Hacini. He is an uncle of Chadli, my young entrepreneur. He is in his seventies, or maybe older. This is a desert village of tents, though I hear radios, and see jeeps in the streets. In Maziba's tent I see a month-old copy of* El Moudjahid, *the one remaining*

French-language newspaper that can be found in Algiers. So I am in luck, and we converse. He understands, finally, what place I am seeking.

"Old," he tells me, in an oddly accented French. "Very old, that religious place. A half day's journey south, in the desert." I feel intoxicated, I tremble. Tonight I shall not be able to sleep.

Monday . . . We left at five this morning in the Ford, borrowed from Chadli. I drive, Maziba beside me. It is already hot, and we sweat in the heat, though it is a dry heat. The road at first is a hard-packed road. By seven o'clock we begin to pass trucks, jeeps, even a pair of bicyclists. It is noon, blazingly hot, when Maziba touches my arm, "Voilà!" And he points to a road off to our left, and I make the turn. We drive now for two hours southwest, under a burning sun. The road has become narrow and vestigial. At last, in the distance, hazily, I see an uneven mound on the desert floor. Maziba mutters something under his breath, then. "Not well-visited, that religious place," he says in his oddly accented French, and he turns a wry, sun-parched face to me. "But for my part, I sometimes . . . Because who knows? Who knows? La possibilité est immense."

Now I tremble again, thinking, Yes! Yes! La possibilité immense.

I drive on. The wind blows swirls of sun-

filtered sand no higher than a man's knees. The mound resolves itself into a group of mud-colored domes.

"The religious place," says Maziba. Now I see there is one large building consisting of three domes: two small domes like arms of the larger, central dome, which has a high arched entrance. I drive up to the entrance, before which squats a figure on a worn fragment of carpet. "The gatekeeper," says Maziba. "To enter, we must pay."

The gatekeeper. I was never to enter that great, domed building after all. Because when I spoke to the gatekeeper, using the French word chercher, *and I saw that he understood, on impulse, I dared to say what I searched for. It was then, looking at me with his sable eyes, he answered me in French, and, in puzzlement, held up his right hand.*

40

Inspector Egan O'Hare hadn't cried since he was eight years old and Billy Gallagher had said, "Only sissies cry," and then, triumphantly seeing the tears, had let go of little Egan O'Hare's wrist after a two-minute wrist burn.

Inspector O'Hare, at his desk in the Ballynagh police station, put down the phone and absentmindedly rubbed his wrist. He swore under his breath.

"What's that, sir?" Sergeant Jimmy Bryson paused in putting on his parka. It was ten in the morning, time for his Monday-morning gassing up of the police car at Duffy's Garage, then his routine cruise around the village.

"That damned Mickey O'Boyle and his *Inquiry!*" So, no surprise that five minutes ago Chief Superintendent Emmet O'Reilly had rung up from Harcourt Square, each word in his overeducated voice an icicle, asking, "Exactly what progress on the Gwathney murder investigation, Egan?"

O'Hare rubbed a hand down his face. For the first time in his twenty-six-year-old career, he felt a chasm at his feet. No proof for his suspicions about Megan O'Faolain and her possibly conniving with Liam Caffrey in John Gwathney's murder. Caffrey himself was still an unknown card, for God's sake! The fax from the Galway police concerning Caffrey's divorce had arrived a half hour ago. It lay on his desk. The report confirmed that Liam Caffrey and his ex-wife had lived apart for four of the past five years with no prospect of reconciliation, as required by the Grounds for Divorce ruling in Ireland. No further information, as yet.

"I'm off." Sergeant Bryson felt for the car keys in his pocket, headed for the door, then stopped. "Someone coming." He was looking through the plate-glass front of the police station. "Her. On that foreign bicycle of hers." He raised his brows, grinning, then jingled the keys and went out. The door slammed behind him.

Ms. Torrey Tunet. Face like something in a Shakespearean tragedy. She was pale, and there were faint blue shadows under her eyes. Had she given up sleeping? She wore jeans and boots and a short, worn-looking sheepskin coat. Red earmuffs and no hat. Her short wavy hair was blown about by the wind.

"Inspector." She dug into her shoulder bag and took out a worn-looking brown suede pocket journal. She put it on his desk. Then she took a loose-leaf notebook from the bag.

She held it a moment, then she sighed and laid that, too, on his desk.

". . . startled by hearing someone behind me, I accidentally brushed the journal and the little address book into my pocket." Ms. Tunet hesitated, flushed. "When I found them later in my pocket, at the cottage, I was going to bring them to you, Inspector. But Roger Flannery stole them from the cottage."

O'Hare felt the beginning of a headache, a throb starting at his temples. He looked at the worn-looking journal on his desk. "But . . . isn't that the journal?"

A slow flush rose in Ms. Tunet's face. "I suspected . . . I had reason to believe it was Roger Flannery who'd stolen . . . who'd taken the journal and address book from my cottage. So next morning, at Gwathney Hall, I . . . I got them back."

"I see." *Stolen them back* would have been more accurate. So Ms. Tunet was still a thief. Once a thief, always a thief. A recidivist. Strange that she could sit there, her gaze meeting his.

"And the address book?" he said dryly. "Where's the address book?"

Ms. Tunet shook her head. "I don't know what happened to it. I lost it, somehow."

Lying again, no doubt. He felt a rising anger. "Ms. Tunet! You've had John

Gwathney's journal in your possession for how long?" He could almost feel his blood pressure rising. It was no good Noreen always telling him he shouldn't let himself get excited. As though he had a choice! Noreen didn't know Ms. Tunet.

Ms. Tunet said unhappily, "Umm . . . a week?" And before he could explode in a rage, she added, "I'd hoped to find something in the journal that would indicate who killed . . . The journal's in Greek, so it was taking me —"

"You mean you expected to find something to clear your friend Megan O'Faolain!" Now he was furious. "That journal should have been in my hands a week ago!" Calm down, calm *down*. He looked at the pocket journal lying on his desk. Shabby, worn, stained. Well-traveled. He leaned back and contemplated Ms. Tunet. "And did you find something, Ms. Tunet, to clear Megan O'Faolain? What *did* you find? The 'real' killer of John Gwathney?"

Ms. Tunet did not look happy. "I found enough to make me think you might want to have a preliminary investigation, one of your 'informals' that in the past have twice revealed a murderer." She got up and shrugged into the sheepskin coat and put her red earmuffs back on. She looked down at the loose-leaf notebook on O'Hare's desk. "I'll be at the cottage. You can let me know."

He watched through the plate glass as she bicycled off, the bicycle wobbling a bit. Then he picked up the loose-leaf notebook.

41

In the old groundsman's cottage, Torrey put peat on the fire, paced from fireplace to couch to desk, looked a dozen times at the clock, ate a peanut butter sandwich, glared helplessly at the telephone, then picked up the extra copy she'd made of John Gwathney's journal and sat down cross-legged on the couch.

On the plane leaving Algiers, I am exhausted but with an excitement I can barely contain. A dozen times I put my hand in my pocket to reassure myself that my tissue-wrapped treasure is there. The gatekeeper thought I was a madman when I asked for it. I can see him now, squatting on that fragment of carpet in the desert sand, a skinny figure in a loin-cloth, he looks up at me. Madman, madman, *his sable eyes are saying, and then he smiles, showing broken blackened teeth, and he nods and holds out his hand, and I put the coins in it and take out my pocket knife —*

The phone rang.
"Ms. Tunet?" It was Inspector O'Hare.

42

"Wednesday morning in Ballynagh?" Cherry wailed. "At the police station? Oh, Roger! Do you *have* to go? That means we can't have lunch at the Shelbourne. And then, the rerun of *Chicago*!" She collapsed onto the cheap old sofa that they weren't taking with them when they moved to Ballsbridge. Everything would be new and expensive. She and Roger had spent hours having meetings with the decorators, two gentlemen who were constantly written up in the decorating magazines. "What's this 'informal' investigative procedure anyway? I've never heard of such a thing."

Roger didn't answer. It was Ms. Torrey Tunet, of course. She had to have gone to Inspector O'Hare with the journal. He cocked his head, suddenly alert. A sound outside?

"What's out there?" Cherry said, for he was at the window, and despite the cold, had flung it up and was craning his neck, looking down.

"The car." He pulled himself back into the room and, shivering, shut the window. "It's okay. I just . . . I had a kind of . . . I had a feeling it was gone." His olive-green Mercedes.

Sergeant Jimmy Bryson crossed off Roger Flannery's name. Then he fed a cookie to Nelson and turned from his desk and looked over at Inspector O'Hare. "I don't see Winifred Moore's name, Inspector. Winifred Moore considers herself John Gwathney's special friend. She had a poem about him in *The Dublin Times* last week. So —"

"So she'd raise holy hell if we didn't demand her attendance? This isn't a goddamned circus, Jimmy. It's an inquiry into a murder!"

"Still, sir."

O'Hare sighed. He hadn't slept last night. He rubbed his eyes. "Right, right. Call her."

Sergeant Bryson picked up the phone, then hesitated. "She'll bring Sheila Flaxton, of course. Telling her not to bring Ms. Flaxton would be like telling the earth to stop orbiting around the moon. Or is it the moon orbiting . . . No, the earth. Like telling the earth —"

"Never mind, Jimmy!"

"Liam?" Megan was calling on the phone from her bedroom, the bedroom she had moved to so many months ago. It faced west and was smaller than the bedroom in the east wing that she had shared with John Gwathney. John, who rose early, had loved to see the sun rise. She had thought often lately, with a sharp pain, of those halcyon days that she and John Gwathney had shared, and how in that room, on that bed, they had made love.

"Sergeant Bryson called me." Liam's baritone voice calmed her, it was so steady. "He called you, too? An informal inquiry, that's all, Megan. That's *all*."

"Pa," Willow said, "it's for you." She brought the phone from the end table, under the hunting print, to her father. At Castle Creedon, there was a blazing fire in the library. Owen Thorpe, in a big leather chair by the row of tall windows, was reading a book about seasonal plantings. A brisk wind rattled the windows. It was the kind of sunny, cold morning that demanded a hot soup for lunch. Willow was still in rather dirty jodhpurs, and a bit of straw was caught in her ponytail, though Buddy, her twin, had done most of the currying. They'd had a wonderful morning canter. Before leaving the stable, they'd shared a cigarette, then rinsed their mouth with the bottle of mouthwash they kept hidden in the empty horse stall along with the pack of cigarettes. They'd discussed the possibility of getting an advance on their allowance and had come into the library to beard the lion.

"Yes?" her father said into the phone, balancing the book on his knees. A minute later, the book about seasonal plantings slid from his lap to the carpet.

"Owen." Their mother was in the doorway. "I've told Mary: barley soup with mushrooms and peas, unless you'd rather —" She stopped; then: "Owen, what is it?" She put a hand to her heart.

"Yes," he said into the phone. "Yes, of course." Carefully, he put down the phone. "Nothing, really, Constance. A Sergeant Bryson, in Wicklow. The John Gwathney murder. Some sort of preliminary investigation in the village of Ballynagh. Wednesday morning, ten o'clock. Our attendance is requested. I —"

"*Our* attendance?"

A nod. "It appears there's a record of John Gwathney visiting Castle Creedon a month before his death." He picked up the book from the floor and said tiredly, "In Sergeant Bryson's words, we may be able 'to contribute information in the Gardaí's pursuit of the case.' And so on." He paused. "And, of course, the reason for John Gwathney's visit to Castle Creedon."

Into a long, puzzling silence, Buddy said, "Wow! Can we come too?"

"*No!*" His father's explosive word made him jump. His father's ordinarily serene face looked suddenly like a stranger's, the way his jaw was clenched.

Buddy looked at Willow and wiggled his eyebrows. Forget about the allowance.

43

At nine-thirty Wednesday morning, a crisp, clear, cold day, Sergeant Jimmy Bryson carried the folding chairs, from the Grogan Sisters Knitting Shop across the street to the Garda station. The Grogan sisters had their weekly knitting-instruction meetings, often referred to as "gossip" meetings, on Fridays, so they didn't need the chairs right then.

Jimmy Bryson made three trips. On his last trip, he suddenly had to leap up onto the curb, though Winifred Moore stepped hard on the brakes of the red Jeep and yelled, "Sorry, Jimmy! Sorry! These damned brakes!"

Inside the station, Sergeant Bryson said to Inspector O'Hare, who was sitting at his desk and staring narrow-eyed into space, "Winifred Moore and her friend Sheila Flaxton are already here. And she's brought Blake Rossiter."

"Hmmm?" O'Hare refocused on Sergeant Bryson. "Not surprising. Rossiter is evaluating old paintings and portraits of Moore ancestors up at Castle Moore. I've heard that Winifred now thinks Rossiter is God. Or similar. Blake Rossiter won't be the only uninvited person to show up. Ms. Rosaleen O'Shea, our local fledgling gossip columnist, will likely come slipping through the door, ears at the ready and tongue set to spice up the facts. And it's anybody's guess who else might appear."

Ten o'clock. They were all here, settling down on the folding chairs that Sergeant Bryson had arranged in rows.

Standing in front of his desk, leaning back, Inspector O'Hare, smiling, said, "Good morning." He stood with one leg crossed against the other, casual, that was the ticket. Unintimidating. Hands in his pockets. Behind him on the desk, within easy reach, lay the objects he'd refer to. He looked over to where, behind the rows of seated people just beside the door, Ms. Torrey Tunet was standing next to the soda machine. Wearing a heavy red sweater, she stood with her legs crossed as casually as his own, hands in the pockets of her jeans. But even from here he could see that her face was pale. He was surprised that she wasn't wearing her peacock bandanna, turquoise and gold. A bit cocky, that bandanna. He'd come to think of it as a symbol of . . . success? luck? He felt a momentary qualm.

It was not his first qualm. It was true that his earlier investigative "informals" had been successful in exposing the guilty. It was, as always, the word "informal," that psychologically misled the guilty into thinking "unofficial," a safe chance to spy out the direction of the investigation.

Nevertheless . . . O'Hare drew a deep breath. Skill was required. This room was spilling over with people who had motives to kill John Gwathney. Never mind the stunning revelation from Gwathney's stained journal pages. It wasn't proof enough. Not *quite* enough. What he must do was to lay a trap that, once sprung, would produce a confession.

Smell of . . . violets? Hyacinths? A woman's perfume. Constance Thorpe from Castle Creedon was in the first row, beside her husband. A gray-blond beautiful woman with a pensive mouth and sky-blue eyes, she was wrapped in a plaid woolen cape that she clutched closed at the throat with one hand, though the room was comfortably warm, Sergeant Bryson having turned up the heat. She'd perhaps gotten chilled during the drive north from Baltimore. Owen Thorpe, in the folding chair beside his wife, was an athletic-looking man in country tweeds and a knitted tie. He was fair-haired and had a square-jawed, tanned face with shadows under tired-looking brown eyes. A muscle in his cheek twitched. On the folding chair beside him, he'd placed a wicker basket that held a thermos and a woman's pale blue cashmere shawl.

Behind the Thorpes sat Winifred Moore in her Australian outback hat. She was flanked on one side by Sheila Flaxton, who looked like a beaky little bird buried in a nest of woolen scarves. On Winifred's other side was Blake Rossiter in a brown suede jacket over a yellow-checked shirt. He looked more like a country squire than an art dealer. His light blue eyes under the sandy brows looked alertly about.

In back of them sat Megan O'Faolain and Liam Caffrey. Megan O'Faolain looked thinner, possibly because of the cranberry-colored jersey dress she wore . . . thin as she had been when, half-starved, she'd hunted hare with a shotgun that late October, six — or was it seven? — years ago. Her dark hair was in a bun at her nape and it made O'Hare think of the word "chaste," which, at the same time, he thought wryly, was hardly fitting. Liam Caffrey, on Megan's left, was in his usual black turtleneck. He met Inspector O'Hare's gaze, and the sardonic lines around his mouth deepened.

On Megan's right was Roger Flannery in an olive-green linen shirt and a tan cashmere jacket. He had thrown his luxurious-looking butter-colored suede coat over the back of his chair. His high freckled forehead shone, and his reddish-brown hair in its ponytail had a polished look.

Inspector O'Hare felt an anticipatory

shiver. He smiled at the waiting faces. "To begin —"

"Sorry! Sorry!" From the back of the room, a giggly kind of apologetic whisper, and Ms. Rosaleen O'Shea tiptoed past the soda machine, looked about, then slid into an empty seat that Sergeant Bryson unfolded beside Blake Rossiter.

Inspector O'Hare took a breath, smiled once more around the room and said, "First. I'd like —"

Nelson barked, a sharp, startled bark. The door had opened again, striking his behind. Two teenaged boys in pea-green fleece jackets and white knitted caps closed the door behind them. No, it was a boy and a girl. "Damn!" the girl said and grabbed Nelson's muzzle in a gentle admonitory way and shook it back and forth. "Shut up, you beast. Put a clamp on it."

A moan from Constance Thorpe. Owen Thorpe said tight-lipped, "I should have drained the petrol from their motorbikes."

There were no more folding chairs. The boy and girl stood beside Torrey Tunet and looked with polite, almost military, attention at Inspector O'Hare.

For a bare instant, O'Hare felt a quaking sensation, a protest. Something in the Bible . . . *The sins of the fathers?* Yet nothing to do but press on. He'd agreed finally with Torrey Tunet, exclude, *exclude,* clear the decks. A stubborn young woman, Ms. Tunet, fighting against believing the obvious. Then, in John Gwathney's journal, that incredible tale, *With my pocket knife I cut off a swatch of the gate-keeper's hair.*

Nevertheless, as promised to the stubborn Ms. Torrey Tunet, who seemed to be casting desperately about for a miracle, he would forge ahead, no deviation, despite the bird in hand. He had an uneasy memory of last year's case, which had involved the admittedly clever Ms. Tunet. So he smiled at the attentive faces before him and cleared his throat.

"I hope that with this informal meeting, and with the concentrated effort of all of you . . . I hope to pull together the events surrounding the death of John Gwathney.

"So, Ms. Megan O'Faolain, if you please."

"Oh!" Megan O'Faolain clasped her hands in her lap and in a low voice, with its touch of the lyric Sligo, told of that terrible evening — of the arrival of Sharon, her little niece, and the horror of finding John Gwathney with his shattered chest. "No, never any threats, Inspector . . . No, John was not a man to make enemies . . . Yes, he had just returned from a research trip abroad . . . The killer frightened off by my return? I can't say, I have no idea . . . I'm sorry."

Silence. Then an unexpected, vehement

whisper from Winifred Moore: "And we think we live in a civilized society! Dominated, of course, by the male sex!" At this outburst, Sheila Flaxton turned her pale blue eyes to the heavens.

"Thank you, Ms. O'Faolain." O'Hare looked over to Roger Flannery in the folding chair on Megan's right. "If you please, Mr. Flannery."

Roger Flannery, fingering a cuff link from which a tiny diamond winked, told of his arrival that night at Gwathney Hall, the shock of it. "Had to be attempted robbery. John Gwathney, the finest of . . . What's that, Inspector, I didn't quite . . . Oh, his will? Yes, I was totally astonished, Inspector, in fact, stunned — John Gwathney leaving me a painting! And it turning out to be worth a million pounds! Staggering, what with it being only a painting of a couple of dogs . . . I'd no idea paintings could be . . . Yes, Inspector, I knew John Gwathney owned a few paintings, I passed them every day, here and there, but can't say I ever really noticed. Worth ten pounds each, for all I knew! Now, of course, I have rather a collection of books on the subject . . . What's that, Inspector? Yes, eight years ago, in Limerick. John found me in rather poor, uh, circumstances, you might say. He straightened me up. I owed John Gwathney a lot, in fact." Unconsciously he ran a hand down the side of his butter-colored suede coat.

At that, somebody snickered. Ms. Rosaleen O'Shea. She even gave Blake Rossiter, in the chair beside her, a slight poke in the ribs.

Inspector O'Hare cast Rosaleen O'Shea a frowning look. A vexing young woman. But no time for that. He leaned back against the desk, his heart beating a little faster. He looked over at Liam Caffrey beside Megan O'Faolain. Liam Caffrey looked attentively back at him, a smile lurking around his sardonic mouth. O'Hare felt a kind of resentment. However, he pushed on.

"Mr. Caffrey, a question or two, if you don't mind."

The room was suddenly dead quiet. Liam Caffrey. Rumors, gossip. Even from here, O'Hare could see a flush rising from Megan's throat, creeping up her face to her brow. Dark hair in a chaste bun, but the lady was anything but chaste. A hand, her left, fluttered to her brow, then fell to her lap.

"Yes, Inspector?" Liam Caffrey's lean face reflected only curiosity.

"The evening that John Gwathney was killed — that evening. Your pottery shop is on the road about two hundred yards' distance from Gwathney Hall." He glanced down at his notes. "I believe in your interview by the Gardaí from Dublin, you reported you may have heard someone going past at around six that evening?"

Liam Caffrey said, "Did I say that? Around that time, six o'clock, I was occupied . . . what with one thing or another." Liam Caffrey leaned suddenly forward, his face had gone dark, his voice was coldly angry. "Inspector! Don't make anything of that incident at the bar in O'Malley's Pub! John Gwathney trying to break my leg with that damned walking stick of his. Deliberate as hell! I —"

"Liam!" Megan O'Faolain's hand was on his arm, her voice begging. "Liam! No! You'll just —"

A whispery young woman's voice from over beside Blake Rossiter said, "Oh, you nasty thing, Mr. Liam Caffrey! John Gwathney was only trying to pay you back! Pay you back for hurting her! I saw the bruises! That time I brought the towels to her room after she came back from visiting you! Lots of times you must've done that to her!"

A stunned silence. Then a groan from Megan O'Faolain, who put up her hands and covered her face. Winifred Moore whispered something about "sadism bearing a close relationship to the arts." There was a swell of outraged murmurs and shocked, appalled looks cast at Liam Caffrey. Inspector O'Hare glanced over at Ms. Torrey Tunet, standing back there beside the soda machine. She looked bewildered.

Then: "Wait a bit!" It was a cry from Roger Flannery. It startled the room into silence. O'Hare, fingering his notes, looked up in surprise. But having gone that far, Roger Flannery only sat back, silent, running a hand nervously over his gleaming hair.

"Mr. Flannery?" Inspector O'Hare frowned; he was feeling sidetracked. He knew where he was going with this investigation, and now, *this*. He felt a warmth at the back of his neck; it always happened when he felt frustrated, held up, impatient. He frowned at Roger Flannery, whose ordinarily pale face now went even paler, and whose brown eyes looked back at him with a kind of desperation.

"If you please, Mr. Flannery. If you have something pertinent . . . But this is an investigation that —"

"Yes! But that's a terrible . . ." Roger Flannery said in a strangled voice. "What she said! That's not true!" He looked around the room, then at Megan O'Faolain. "Liam Caffrey never beat Megan. It was . . . It was John Gwathney who beat her. John started beating Megan even before" — Flannery jerked his head toward Liam Caffrey — "before she ever met *him!*"

"Roger! Don't! *Please!*" Megan O'Faolain's voice was a cry, a desperate plea. In the chair beside him, she reached out and grasped his arm, but he shook himself free. "*Yes*, Megan! Always trying to excuse him! No more excuses!"

Inspector O'Hare rocked back on his heels with surprise, looked in disbelief at Roger Flannery. "Mr. Flannery! You realize that such accusations —"

"Of course!" Flannery was breathing hard. Then, taking an uneven breath: "I don't know how they got to John, those Dublin bastards. Or maybe he went looking for it, experimenting. In his travels, he'd been in strange places where he tried hallucinatory drugs, I knew that. We'd even chatted about it. But now, *now* . . . Drug-inspired fantasies, out of control. He started imagining that Megan was cheating on him with lovers. It was frightening. I'd find scribbled notes, crumpled bits of paper, even in the files: *Each time she lies with a different man! I know it! This time it is a boy named Jack, she likes them young . . . I won't beat her if she'll confess. But she won't confess. Liar, liar, liar! I will burn my initials on her breasts. Then they'll know whom she belongs to.*"

A mewling sound, like an injured cat, from Sheila Flaxton; but Roger Flannery pressed on: "*She says I am sick, that I need help. I don't like to make her cry. But I have to! I will beat the truth out of her. I will beat her until she confesses! . . . She has called them again. I don't want help.*"

Roger Flannery sank back, exhausted. The neck of his olive-green shirt was dark with sweat. He took a deep breath. "John would go from Mr. Hyde back to Dr. Jekyll and become the real, decent, kind John Gwathney. Ninety percent of the time he was the brilliant, serious historian, then . . ." Roger spread his hands. "We never knew. It was frightening. One night, three or four days before John returned to Gwathney Hall, Megan took the drugs from his bathroom cabinet. She brought them to me, she was afraid that when he got back, he'd start right away . . . So I hid them in my rooms at Gwathney Hall. I still have them. Three packets. Worth a fortune." He fingered a cuff, a diamond cuff link winked. "Been meaning to turn them over to . . . uh, the right department at Dublin Castle. Or is it Harcourt Square? But, what with one thing and another . . ."

The room was quiet. Inspector O'Hare felt he had been caught in a maelstrom and tossed about to land in a different place. Shock and disillusionment, tragedy in Flannery's revelation about John Gwathney, with its ring of truth. Megan O'Faolain sitting there, staring ahead, hands clasped in her lap.

As for Flannery . . . White horse, dark horse. Devious. Much unknown.

"Thank you, Mr. Flannery." Inspector O'Hare smiled at Roger Flannery. *All in good time, Mr. Flannery.* And he moved a hand to the desk behind him and touched the folder in which he had placed Ms. Torrey's translation along with John Gwathney's journal in Greek, that journal stolen from Torrey Tunet's cottage by Roger Flannery.

44

"Mr. Owen Thorpe, if you please." Inspector O'Hare's voice was friendly, courteous. "Sorry to have brought you and your wife all this way from Baltimore, Mr. Thorpe. But you may be of help in this inquiry."

Standing beside the soda machine at the back of the room, Torrey felt something like an icicle slide down her back. She reached inside her shoulder bag and felt her copy of the translation of John Gwathney's journal. She hated what was about to happen; it sickened her. Admit it: she'd persuaded Inspector O'Hare to have this inquiry in the hope of discovering John Gwathney's killer among those who had *already* in the last hour been called on: Roger Flannery, evasive, thieving, now so rich, through John Gwathney's will, and claiming that Gwathney had destroyed his manuscript, burned it.

As for Liam Caffrey, over there beside Megan O'Faolain, all she knew, in frustration, was that through John Gwathney's death he was gaining Megan O'Faolain and the Gwathney Hall estate.

And now, alas, Owen Thorpe. She wanted to weep. She was seeing the scratched, almost illegible words in Greek in the battered pocket journal: *I had the relic from Castle Creedon. Over three hundred years! What I am accomplishing is not miraculous, but the result of research. The genetic fault in the Creedon family line. Is it any wonder I am wild with excitement? The child! The child! In the desert I found what I was searching for.*

"Cigarette?" A shapely, grubby hand holding out a pack of cigarettes. Willow, in her pea-green fleece jacket, lovely, mischievous face grinning. Torrey shook her head. "No, thanks, strictly forbidden in the police station. Sergeant Bryson will draw and quarter you." Careless choice of words. Again that icicle down her back. She looked at Inspector O'Hare standing in front of his desk and smiling at Owen Thorpe.

"Now, let's see." Inspector O'Hare looked down at his notes. "Ah, yes. It appears, Mr. Thorpe, that early in September, John Gwathney visited you at Castle Creedon. The purpose of his visit, Mr. Thorpe, if you don't mind?"

"Not at all." A baritone voice, cultivated, a shade weary. Owen Thorpe, in tweed jacket and knitted tie, sat at ease, his legs crossed. Brown-eyed, fair-haired, with a square-jawed, tanned face, he had the outdoors look of a sportsman who enjoyed the seasons. "Mr. Gwathney told us he was researching a history of castles in the area. It was for a book he was writing." Owen Thorpe recrossed his legs. "And since Castle Creedon dates from the late fifteenth century . . ." Owen Thorpe shrugged. "So we showed him about."

"And historically? Castle Creedon . . . The visit was helpful to Mr. Gwathney historically?"

Owen Thorpe said, "I . . . Possibly." He hesitated. "He was interested in a few relics we keep in a glass case in the north tower, sixteenth century, dating from before my wife's family purchased the property in the seventeen hundreds. Such Castle Creedon relics are of interest to tour groups. We open the castle and the gardens to the public on Thursdays one month of the year."

"I see. Historic." Inspector O'Hare nodded. He reached around behind him and picked up the translation of John Gwathney's journal. "I have here John Gwathney's handwritten notes about his projected book. The working title is *The Raid of Baltimore*. Historically known as *The Sack of Baltimore*. The book would be about the kidnapping of people in Baltimore by Algerian pirates in sixteen-thirty-one who were taken to North Africa as slaves. Over one hundred people were kidnapped. They were never heard of again. Among them were Desmond and Celia Creedon and their six-year-old child, a girl."

From Sheila Flaxton came a horrified

"How *dreadful!*" followed by a fit of coughing. Winifred Moore exasperatedly pounded on Ms. Flaxton's shawl-wrapped back.

Inspector O'Hare, pressing a finger to his lips, gazed thoughtfully at Owen Thorpe, who involuntarily had put an arm protectively along the back of his wife's chair.

"Tragic," O'Hare said, "tragic." He glanced down at his notes, then up again at Owen Thorpe. Torrey went tense. The exultant words scratched so deeply, excitedly into the journal, *The genetic fault in the Creedon family line: the thumb and three fingers of the right hand, the missing little finger. Yes, yes!*

Inspector O'Hare, leaning a little forward, said, "It appears, Mr. Thorpe, that John Gwathney paid a *second* visit to Castle Creedon." He paused. "That was in October. Only two days before his death. Perhaps you can contribute valuable information. Concerning, say, Mr. Gwathney's emotional state. Did he appear disturbed? And so on." Again he paused. "And, of course, what was the reason for his *second* visit to Castle Creedon?"

The wall clock behind Inspector O'Hare's desk struck the noontime hour: twelve hollow-sounding chimes. Not a rustle, not a sound, only a waiting silence; and despite the closed door, the delicious smell from

207

Finney's across the street, the Wednesday Pot-Roast Special, subversively invaded the room.

"Yes, Inspector. John Gwathney's second visit." Owen Thorpe's baritone voice sounded weary. "Anything I can possibly contribute. However, the trip from Baltimore was exhausting, particularly to my wife. She's just getting over the flu, so it was especially . . . We're plebeian at Castle Creedon, we lunch at noon. So on my wife's account . . ." He paused. ". . . if that's agreeable?"

Inspector O'Hare glanced at Constance Thorpe, who still clutched the plaid cape to her throat. Her head drooped tiredly to one side. Strands of fair hair almost obscured the gleam of a pearl earring.

"By all means." Inspector O'Hare smiled around the room. "An hour's intermission is certainly in order."

No hurry now. Alone with only Sergeant Bryson, who was picking up candy wrappers from under one of the chairs, O'Hare laid the translated journal back on the desk. The net would drop, the killer trapped. Triumphant, he'd tried to catch Ms. Tunet's eye, but she'd slipped out the door, neglecting even to give Nelson one of the dog biscuits she usually carried.

Admit it, he owed Ms. Tunet. Her dereliction in holding on to John Gwathney's journal was outrageous. Yet she'd put the translation into his hands. Therefore he, Inspector Egan O'Hare, and not Chief Superintendent Emmet O'Reilly's staff at Dublin Castle, would reveal the killer of John Gwathney. Now, for the first time in his career, he regretted the absence of the press. And photographers. Ah, well.

"The pot roast?" Sergeant Bryson was beside him.

O'Hare nodded. "With extra noodles."

45

In the silver Jaguar heading south from Belfast on N1, Jasper was reaching the outskirts of Dublin when his cell phone buzzed. He clicked it on and heard "Jasper?" in the low, husky voice that had enchanted him the first time he'd heard it two years ago at the Abbey Theatre, when the young woman with the black-lashed gray eyes and cadet stance had said, "I believe that's *my* seat," and waved her ticket stub at him, and he'd apologized and moved over one seat. The play was Synge's *Playboy of the Western World*, and he'd seen it through a haze, maybe already half in love.

Now, driving on the N1, he glanced at the dashboard clock. Five minutes past twelve. "Torrey? I'm in listening position."

She told him then: Roger Flannery's revelations of John Gwathney drugs and consequent brutality to Megan. "Now, at one o'clock, Inspector O'Hare will . . . will — oh, damn it! He can hardly wait to pounce, with what he's learned from John Gwathney's journal." She paused; then, sadly, in frustration: "Castle Creedon. The Thorpes. It near breaks my heart. That gentle Constance

Thorpe! And there's a pair of twins, a boy and a girl . . ."

"Breaks your heart? We can't have that. It'll ruin your appetite." He was thinking hard. He glanced at the speedometer, then at the rearview mirror, and pressed down on the gas. One possibility. Only one. It might help. Or maybe not.

"Jasper? You there?"

"I'm here. I'll see you in Ballynagh almost before you hang up."

On Pearse Street in Dublin, he parked illegally, risking it, and rang the bell of the upstairs flat with the name plate of "R. Flannery." The buzzer sounded without question, and he went up.

"Oh! I was expecting . . ." At the open door of the flat, a young woman in black pants and a black-and-white-striped sweater blinked startled blue eyes at him. She had a charming, saucy face and red hair in ringlets. "I was expecting the wallpaper man. From Devon's."

"Sorry, miss. Not from Devon's. I'm from Keady's. Picking up a package for Mr. Flannery. To deliver to him in Ballynagh. Rather a rush, miss."

"A *package?* Roger never —"

"Urgent, Mr. Flannery thought he'd put it in his car, but he'd left it in his" — it was a risk, and he took it — "in his bureau drawer."

211

"Well . . . all right. Just a minute. I'll look."

In the small front room, waiting, he heard a drawer open, then another . . . and another. And another.

Then, pretty face flushed and annoyed, the young woman appeared in the doorway "Is *this* it? It's the only package." She held out a bulky, rather dirty, ten-by-thirteen envelope.

"Yes," Jasper said, "that's it."

46

Michael McIntyre, at his lunchtime window seat in O'Malley's Pub, looked up from the "Shipping News" column as the door opened. Megan O'Faolain and Liam Caffrey. A chin-up lady, face flushing at the sudden silence from the fellows at the bar as they turned and looked at her. Ho! He knew those looks. In ports from Madagascar to the West Indies, sailors looked at certain ladies that way, ladies for knowing intimately if you had the price, or sometimes even only the looks. He himself had had the price, and more than once, at twenty-five, had done fine with just the looks. Smoky rooms, silks and smell of musk, duffel bag tossed in a corner. Skin like satin. Memories, at seventy-six. He lifted his pint to himself and smiled. Megan O'Faolain and Caffrey took a table way at the back, away from the bar, where it was more private. Intimate.

And here came ponytailed Roger Flannery along with that older chap, Rossiter, the art-dealer fellow. Hah! Rossiter was no doubt cozening up to Flannery with a bit of business in mind. Commissions on selling Flannery more paintings. Hah! Money in it.

Why not? Rossiter lived well. Deliveries of fancy wines from Dougherty's, prime meats from O'Curry's. Captain of his ship.

McIntyre rattled the newspaper, ruffled his rampant white hair and looked hopefully out the window. Farther down Butler Street, folks were leaving the police station for lunch. It was one of Egan O'Hare's "informals," as he called them. There went Winifred Moore, a frigate in full sail, trailed by Ms. Flaxton, her fragile "companion." They crossed the street to Finney's. Other folks followed. Pair of boy twins. Or girls? But where was *she*, Ms. Torrey Tunet, who jumped rope in the dead of night? Ms. Tunet of the gray eyes and flower mouth and the peacock bandanna? Ms. Tunet who, buying an apple across the street at Coyle's market, couldn't resist biting into it at once, standing there in jeans and jumper, or leaning on her bike. Where was *she?*

At Finney's, at ten minutes past noon, Winifred Moore cut into her pot roast, took a satisfying bite, and looked around. Sheila, across from her, unwrapped from her layers of woolen shawls, experimentally sipped a spoonful of barley soup. Dennis Finney had the fire going, and the smoky smell of the firewood made the crowded room extra cozy in a companionable, even family-like, way.

"There are the Thorpes and their progeny," Winifred said, "just coming in. What's *that*

214

all about? O'Hare asking them to come all the way from Baltimore!"

Owen and Constance Thorpe and their teenaged twins were settling down at a table near the fire. The twins shrugged out of their jackets. The girl twin took off her white knitted cap. Her long fair hair had a narrow braid down each side of her forehead as far as her chin. She caught Winifred's glance and gave her a puckish grin.

The restaurant door opened again, and then, caught by the wind, slammed shut. Torrey Tunet, windblown, stood looking about. Every table was taken.

"Over here!" Winifred shoved a chair out with her booted foot and waved Torrey over, meanwhile under her breath muttering to Sheila, "My God! She looks like a Dickens orphan!"

Pale, looking dispirited, and obviously forcing a smile, Torrey collapsed into one of the two empty chairs. A strand of wool had come loose at the cuff of her red jumper, and unthinkingly she twisted and rolled it between thumb and forefinger.

"I *know*," Winifred said with feeling, but nevertheless cutting into her pot roast, "dreadful! Roger Flannery's revelation about John Gwathney falling into that terrible trap. Drugs! Sick fantasies, physical cruelty."

"Yes." Torrey's fingers still twisted the strand of wool.

"Mam?" Alice, Finney's oldest, was at Torrey's shoulder, pad in hand, pencil at the ready.

"A pot of tea, please, Alice. And a plate of biscuits. That's all. Thanks." Torrey let go of the loose strand of wool. She reached down into her shoulder bag that rested on the floor and took out a bar of chocolate. She looked at it, then dropped it back into the bag.

"I miss John Gwathney," Winifred said. "Our afternoon siestas. We both drank whiskey neat." She rested her fork on the plate. "John enjoyed visiting me at Castle Moore. He said the castle was built on the site of an ancient fort. But he never invited me to Gwathney Hall. He wasn't keen on visitors."

"But you *did* go to Gwathney Hall!" Sheila said. "Remember? That time I had those awful shingles. And you went *anyway*."

"But I went just to return a book he'd lent me," Winifred said. She watched Alice set down the plate of cookies and pot of tea before Torrey. "He'd been edgy about letting that book out of his hands. A first edition, Irish mythology, a half dozen paragraphs in it about Queen Maeve that I wanted to go over.

"When I got to Gwathney Hall, John was out on the steps saying good-bye to a city-dressed chap who looked rather like a sprite. A Mr. Bendersford. We shook hands. John was . . . all frowning eyebrows. A thunder-cloud! Angry about something. 'I'd like to strangle Clewes and Company!' he said to Mr. Bendersford. At that, Mr. Bendersford gave a little laugh and said, 'Go to it!' and 'Thanks for the autographs.' And he got into his little mini and went off. Those piddling little cars! Give me a Jeep anytime!"

Twenty minutes later, Torrey stood on the curb outside Finney's. Bendersford. Some-thing . . . something remembered. Benders-ford. Yes. She could see Megan O'Faolain smiling at her that afternoon she'd returned the soft-as-thistledown apricot-colored scarf that Megan had forgotten at Castle Moore.

Bendersford. Megan saying he'd stopped at Gwathney Hall on his way to Waterford, something about an autograph for his young nephew. Megan smiling, saying, *I made a lob-ster lunch. It was lovely, we had a white wine. I was happy to see John so relaxed. So buoyant.*

On the curb, Torrey frowned. Something . . . off. Winifred Moore, minutes ago in Finney's saying that on the steps outside, John was saying good-bye to Mr. Benders-ford. He was angry . . . *all frowning eyebrows. A thundercloud . . . "I'd like to strangle Clewes and Company!"* And then from Bendersford: *"Go to it!"*

Odd. It didn't tally. Unless . . . unless something had happened right after that

happy lobster lunch. Something that had in-
furiated John Gwathney.

Torrey stood a moment, biting a fingernail.
And slowly she was beginning to remember
something else, something glimpsed. A color.
Wine-red. No, that was something worn.
That wasn't it. It was something else, some-
thing square, olive-green. *Olive-green.* A
carton, with an address. Her eyes widened.
She blew out a breath and stood very still.
Then, heart pounding, she unzipped her
shoulder bag and took out her cell phone.

Dublin information; she gave the name and
waited. It was windy, dry leaves were skit-
tering down Butler Street; she was chilled,
she should have worn a heavier sweater, a
jumper, as they called it here. Rosaleen
O'Shea came by and hesitated, but Torrey
looked skyward and, thankfully, Rosaleen
O'Shea took the hint and went on up the
street. An instant later, in Dublin, someone
picked up the ringing phone.

Five minutes later, Torrey clicked off her
cell phone. Her blood was pounding. She felt
incredibly alive. She looked at her watch.
Thirty-five minutes before one o'clock. Time!
She needed time!

"Hey. Hello!" Willow, the Thorpe girl twin,
had come out of Finney's. Lovely, mischievous face, white knitted hat, pea-green fleece
jacket. "Quite something, this village. Antedi-

luvian. I'll have a look about. Then back to the Inquisition, conducted by that cute inspector who's getting a bit corpulent. But he puts on a good show. Catch a murderer. God knows why we Thorpes were invited."

Torrey didn't even hesitate before she asked Willow right out, it mattered that much.

Willow, face alight, gave it less than a minute before she agreed.

47

Ten minutes past one. Murmur of voices as everyone settled again on the folding chairs. Crackle of cellophane as Rosaleen O'Shea offered a bag of mints to Blake Rossiter beside her. Sheila Flaxton had brought bottled water; there was a hiss as she twisted off the cap.

Inspector O'Hare, standing beside his desk, cast a questioning glance at Sergeant Bryson, who shook his head, equally puzzled. Ms. Tunet was missing. O'Hare frowned, then shrugged. She'd given him John Gwathney's journal. If she was unhappy about its contents, unwilling to be on hand for the ugly revelation, that was hardly his affair. His glance skimmed across Owen Thorpe in the front row.

Constance Thorpe, who was sitting with one hand on her husband's tweed-clad arm, leaned around to Buddy, who had removed the wicker basket to sit beside his father. "Where's Willow?"

Buddy shrugged. "Don't know. Gone off. Viewing the countryside." Gone off with that dishy American, Ms. Tunet, on the back of her motorbike. Not enough cushioning. If they went far, Ms. Tunet would have a sore behind.

Inspector O'Hare cleared his throat, smiled around the room, then looked again at Owen Thorpe.

"Mr. Thorpe? Let's see, now. October. Two days before John Gwathney's death. His second visit to Castle Creedon. If you could . . ." He waited.

"Absolutely, Inspector!" Owen Thorpe's voice was clear, resonant. He sat relaxed, one leg crossed over the other, his tanned face with the shadows under his dark eyes looked frankly back at Inspector O'Hare. "Anything I can . . . Mid-morning, maybe half ten, brisk weather, I'd just come up from a visit to the stables. Found Constance in the morning room providing John Gwathney with a cup of tea. He was doing further historical research in the area." Owen Thorpe, recalling, tapped fingers on his tweed-clad knee. "We had a bit of friendly chitchat. There was nothing more Constance or I could contribute historically. We'd shot our bolt first time around."

"So, then . . . ?" Inspector O'Hare said.

Owen Thorpe looked surprised. "So then Gwathney had a biscuit or two with his tea, and off he went. Foraging, likely, for more bits and pieces of research around the harbor. Constance was quite impressed. She'd read a book or two of Gwathney's. Not my style."

"Ah." O'Hare felt a kind of admiration mixed with incredulity at the depravity of mankind. He said, gently, thinking, why squeeze the bird in hand, "Unfortunately, Gwathney destroyed his manuscript. His reason is unknown."

Owen Thorpe said agreeably, "Possibly Mr. Gwathney was a perfectionist. Perhaps he felt the projected work not quite up to . . . However."

"However," O'Hare went on, acknowledging Owen Thorpe's contribution with a nod, "in regard to this investigation, Gwathney left a journal of his research into *The Raid of Baltimore.*" He reached around to the desk behind him and picked up the journal. "I have here John Gwathney's journal —"

A startled cry from Roger Flannery, then something rattled to the floor. Roger Flannery bent over and his head was lost to view as he rooted around the floor, then came up, face flushed, ponytail awry, his silver pen in hand. He sat back and stared at the journal.

O'Hare managed to conceal a smile and went on.

"This journal is John Gwathney's research notes for his book on *The Raid of Baltimore.*" He paused and looked from face to face. "He wrote it in Greek, possibly for privacy, who knows? In any case, it recounts John Gwathney's research in Baltimore, and then in Algeria, his attempts to trace the kidnapped people who were sold into slavery. And . . . his results."

Dead quiet in the room. Fascinated faces, guarded faces. Against the windowpanes a pinpoint scattering of rain. Inspector O'Hare felt a pounding of blood in his ears. He said, "There are passages here that are, in fact, relevant to John Gwathney's death at Gwathney Hall."

Gasps, and a half-hysterical giggle from Ms. Rosaleen O'Shea.

O'Hare wished that the door would open and Ms. Torrey Tunet would appear. He owed her. A pity that she wasn't here to witness the fruits of her —

The door opened. Not Ms. Tunet, but Jasper Shaw, Ms. Tunet's whatever-you-call-it. Lover. Overcoat with the collar up. Mr. Shaw slicked rain from his hair and stood just inside the door beside the soda machine looking about, likely for Ms. Tunet.

O'Hare put down John Gwathney's journal. He picked up Torrey Tunet's notebook with the translation. He had spent half the night marking salient passages with a red pencil. He cleared his throat.

The rain stopped, then started again, as he read. Tattered old documents in an archive in Algiers, a sudden high excitement, *"One child deemed less valuable, having only four fingers of the right hand, the little finger missing, so was bought at a cheaper price by a Berber sect.*"

He read on. The desert, the religious place, "*. . . the gatekeeper, squatting on a fragment of carpet in the desert sand, he holds out his hand and I put the coins in it and take out my pocket knife . . .*"

Someone, Constance Thorpe, cried out, then put a hand quickly over her mouth.

O'Hare, aware, read on, one paragraph after another, five minutes, ten minutes. From the listeners, now and again a gasp or sigh. He turned a page.

"*I was hardly off the plane in Dublin when I drove south to Cork and reached Baltimore and for the first time set foot in Castle Creedon. 'Historical research,' I told the Thorpes, introducing myself. And God knows, it was true! They showed me about, the usual tourist visit: old Creedon portraits and heirlooms. I evinced interest in the architecture of the tower rooms, and they kindly left me to wander around a bit on my own. I managed to pocket a hairbrush from a glass case.*"

O'Hare paused. To his amazement, he had a sudden feeling of sympathy for the Thorpe family. Or, rather, it was pity for the gentle-faced Constance Thorpe and for the boy beside Owen Thorpe, that red-cheeked twin who was gazing at him, puzzled and fascinated. As for Owen Thorpe, sitting there apparently so relaxed, fingers tapping on one knee — all murders were ugly, but the killing at Gwathney Hall with a shotgun . . . O'Hare read on: *"Six days on edge! At last, this morning, the report from the Institute. I can barely take it in! I walk back and forth between desk and window! What I have accomplished is not miraculous, it is the result of brilliant research. After three hundred years,* this!*"*

Inspector O'Hare looked up. "John Gwathney wrote the next entry, his final entry, a week before he was murdered."

Indrawn breaths. Sergeant Jimmy Bryson, beside the soda machine near the door, crossed his arms and cast a glance over the listeners. Last night, Inspector O'Hare had briefed him; he knew the contents of John Gwathney's journal.

Inspector O'Hare continued:

"I have finished the manuscript. It will be my most successful book yet. How can it not be!

"Bringing with me the report from the Institute, I drove south to Baltimore and paid a second visit to Castle Creedon. And there, in that drawing room with its carvings of shields and swords over the fireplace, I told Constance and Owen Thorpe first of my research of the history of Castle Creedon following the Raid of Baltimore, and how Castle Creedon, falling into ruin, had been arbitrarily annexed by the powerful O'Driscoll family in the area, a family who had no legal claim to Castle Creedon. This, as the Thorpes knew, was the family from whom Con-

225

stance Thorpe's ancestors had, a hundred years later, bought Castle Creedon.

"Then, regretfully, with sympathy for Constance and Owen Thorpe, I told them of the genetic fault in the Creedon family, and the DNA results of my desert research in Algeria. And I told them that next week I would be going back to Alergia, to that monastery, and would return to Gwathney Hall bringing with me the Algerian gatekeeper, a descendant of that long-ago enslaved Creedon child.

"Who was the rightful owner of Castle Creedon? Constance and Owen Thorpe? Or that Algerian gatekeeper, descendant of the kidnapped child? I let the Thorpes know that it would be up to the courts to decide.

"Constance Thorpe wept. Owen Thorpe stood with his hand on her shoulder. He looked like a knight, regardless of his Scotch-plaid jacket. I felt sorry for them."

Inspector O'Hare closed Torrey Tunet's translation of John Gwathney's journal. A swelling murmur of excitement, creak of chairs as the listeners strained to catch a glimpse of Owen and Constance Thorpe in the front row. Whispers, exclamations, shivers; then a waiting, a silence, the only sound the spatter of rain on the windowpanes.

Inspector O'Hare cleared his throat. He looked with kindly sympathy at Owen and Constance Thorpe. "Undoubtedly quite a shock, Mr. Thorpe, that second visit from John Gwathney."

Owen Thorpe nodded. "Indeed." His tanned face with the shadows under his dark eyes looked no more than deeply interested. But his lips had gone white.

O'Hare said, "If, in the courts, it came to any question of enmity toward John Gwathney, or that you might have had an interest in preventing the publication of —"

Owen Thorpe gave a short, ironic laugh. "As of course it would, Inspector! The possibility, the *implication,* of the court, that I might've been responsible for John Gwathney's death! To make sure of not losing Castle Creedon to a Berber gate-keeper!" He ran a hand through his graying fair hair. "God help me!"

O'Hare managed a sympathetic shake of his head. "But undoubtedly, Mr. Thorpe, you can account for where you were on the evening of John Gwathney's death."

"Certainly! And right here, right now, in this Ballynagh police station, if you like!" Owen Thorpe's tone was indulgent. He gave a short laugh. "I was at a horse fair in Ennis. There wasn't a horse I liked well enough. Nothing with a decent . . . So I didn't . . ." He frowned. His voice died. He reached over and took Constance Thorpe's hand and held it tightly. "So I didn't buy."

O'Hare smiled, a friendly smile. "But of

course you'd have been seen at the Ennis fair by acquaintances . . . breeders. The like."

"In fact, not, Inspector. No one I knew." Owen Thorpe, frowning, contemplated Inspector O'Hare. Then he smiled. "Inspector, considering that John Gwathney's manuscript would anyway be published soon after his death — that book with its astounding tale about the Castle Creedon child — what good would John Gwathney's death do the Thorpe family? Absurd on the face of it, Inspector. Wouldn't you agree?" And Owen Thorpe's dark eyes smiled at Inspector O'Hare. "The ownership case of Castle Creedon would anyway go to the courts."

For an instant, O'Hare felt a touch of uncertainty.

"Or perhaps, Inspector," Owen Thorpe went on ironically, "one might theorize that when I'd done the dastardly deed, I intended to steal John Gwathney's manuscript and destroy it? . . . Unaware, as we later learned from Mr. Flannery's interview with RTE, that John Gwathney had *already* destroyed the manuscript."

O'Hare had a passing vision of a clever genie let out of a bottle and rising in a swirl of smoke to confound him. He said tightly, "All kinds of theories are possible, Mr. Thorpe. For instance, that you *intended* to destroy the manuscript but fled when Megan

O'Faolain, who had left Gwathney Hall to meet her little niece, Sharon, returned for her jumper." He smiled at Owen Thorpe. "In that case, what an immense relief you would have felt in learning next day on RTE that the manuscript no longer existed!"

"Stop it! *Stop* it!" Constance Thorpe put her hands to her temples and shook her head from side to side; her satiny gray-blond hair falling across her fingers. "This nightmare! This theorizing!"

Murmurs and coughs. Sheila Flaxton patted her heart, Winifred Moore lit a cigarette, giving a defiant look at Sergeant Jimmy Bryson, who pretended not to see. Then, from beside Sergeant Bryson, near the soda machine, a hearty baritone voice: "Inspector!"

Heads turned. Everybody watched Jasper Shaw walk down the side of the room.

Reaching Inspector O'Hare, he said, "This might interest you, Inspector," and Jasper Shaw drew something from a big dirty envelope. It was a two-inch-thick manuscript. Uneven pages, the whole bundle held together by a wide rubber band.

"*No!*" Roger Flannery was on his feet, glaring at Jasper Shaw, his face furious: "You've been to Pearse Street!"

"Tut-tut, as they say in books." Jasper Shaw was grinning. "Let's say I 'retrieved' a bit of evidence from your flat."

Inspector O'Hare held the manuscript. He looked down at the top page. In a jagged handwriting was the word *Final*.

48

Inspector O'Hare, holding the manuscript, felt dazed. He rubbed a finger along the rubber band. In bewilderment, he looked questioningly at Jasper Shaw, who grinned. "The scenario, Inspector? Like this: Ms. Tunet by chance saw John Gwathney's manuscript in his studio the day after he was killed."

Slowly, O'Hare took it in. He felt a chill. "The day *after* he . . . ?"

"Amazing, isn't it, Inspector, that despite Mr. Flannery's sad tale to the press that John Gwathney had destroyed his manuscript, here it turns up, whole and hearty — if a bit disheveled — in Mr. Flannery's possession." Jasper Shaw was still grinning.

Inspector O'Hare stared at Shaw's long, humorous face. Then he turned and put the manuscript down on his desk. Shock and outrage were building in him; he hardly knew which took precedence. He turned back and looked at what seemed to him a hundred startled and expectant faces. Slowly, outrage gave way to a sense of elation. Wasn't this a dispensation from the gods, after all? Gwathney's manuscript was an unexpected windfall. Its pages would help provide a case against Gwathney's murderer, who was sitting there holding his wife Constance's hand tightly in his.

Inspector O'Hare smiled. His gaze sought out Roger Flannery, ponytailed, devious, and caught out. "Precisely why, Mr. Flannery, did you appropriate John Gwathney's manuscript —"

"Swipe," someone murmured. Buddy Thorpe.

"— and lie to the press?"

No answer. Roger Flannery only sank farther back against his luxurious coat.

O'Hare, every instant feeling more secure in the saddle, said crisply, "Exactly why, Mr. Flannery? Please make that clear to me."

No answer.

"Might I suggest, Mr. Flannery, that you planned a use for the manuscript?"

Roger Flannery did not look well. He nodded.

"Let's say . . . A trip to Castle Creedon, Mr. Flannery? A visit to Owen Thorpe?"

Again, no answer. Only a sharply indrawn breath.

"Perhaps, Mr. Flannery, it occurred to you that Owen Thorpe might like to have that manuscript?" O'Hare leaned forward. "For a price, Mr. Flannery?"

Roger Flannery hesitated, then nodded.

"A *big* price, Mr. Flannery?"

"A price worth it to him!" Abruptly Roger Flannery sat up straight and cried out with sudden passion, "Why not? Why should the Thorpe family lose Castle Creedon to some beggar-type Algerian gatekeeper who wouldn't know what to do with it anyway! Just because he has a missing little finger!"

Roger Flannery, face still flushed at the unfairness of life, sank back. Sergeant Jimmy Bryson, arms folded, gave a nod of agreement, then frowned in embarrassment and fed a cookie to Nelson. A gust of wind sent a heavier beating of rain on the window-panes. Then, from among the listeners, a woman's voice, a throaty contralto, said,

"But it wouldn't have! Castle Creedon wouldn't have gone to that Algerian gate-keeper!"

49

It was Megan O'Faolain. Head up, eyes wide, she repeated, "It *wouldn't* have! Because, of course . . . No way I could have known! Not *then*." She worried one of the pearl buttons on her plum-colored silk shirt and it came off in her hand. She sat turning it over and over.

"An Algerian gatekeeper! It meant nothing to me. John was . . . was dead, and at once there were the television crews and all sorts of phone calls coming in. Bills were piling up, and still the usual mail, questions of book rights, letters from fans. Roger — Mr. Flannery — had quite disappeared into Dublin, a girl, I think. So I tried to handle the mail myself.

"That unfamiliar stamp. The letter was so . . . so sweet, so gentle; and such a poor attempt at English, all mixed up with French. About a gatekeeper, elderly, who had suffered an embolism and died. It was signed simply 'Maziba.' "

Megan's hand on the pearl button went still. "The stamp was Algerian."

From the listeners, something like a giant indrawn breath.

★ ★ ★

Inspector O'Hare refrained from looking at Owen Thorpe. It was too ironical that in desperation to save Castle Creedon, Owen Thorpe had needlessly murdered John Gwathney.

The lights flickered, there came a flash of lightning, then a crack of thunder and a heavier spattering of rain against the windows. Simultaneously, the station door opened and two figures appeared.

"*Damn!* It'll shrink my cap!" And Willow, coming in, snatched off her white knitted cap. "*You* again!" she said, stumbling over Nelson. On Willow's heels was Ms. Torrey Tunet. Her brilliant peacock bandanna bound her dark hair and the geranium color was high in her cheeks. She looked, in Winifred Moore's estimation, extraordinarily unlike the Dickens orphan she'd resembled at lunchtime in Finney's. Hugging her outsized canvas shoulder bag to her chest, she gave Jasper Shaw a startled glance and came down the side of the room to where he stood with Inspector O'Hare. "Jasper! I tried — never mind!"

She dropped her shoulder bag beside Inspector O'Hare's desk and looked around. Constance Thorpe, pale and with bitten-off lipstick, sat matching her thumbs. Roger Flannery, arms folded, was staring down at his shoes. Megan O'Faolain was flinching

235

away from Blake Rossiter's overly solicitous attempt to adjust her cashmere scarf, which had slipped from her shoulders. Sergeant Jimmy Bryson was conspicuously ignoring Winifred Moore, who was lighting another cigarette. Ms. Rosaleen O'Shea was on her cell phone, her eyes wide.

"Inspector!" Torrey took a deep breath. "I have —" She broke off. She was staring at the bundle of manuscript on his desk. She reached out a hand and touched the manuscript, then gave a soft, incredulous laugh. She looked at Jasper Shaw and said, "You're wearing that awful striped sweater again."

Owen Thorpe said, "Inspector." He was seated so close that Torrey could see his hand tremble as he ran it through his fair hair. "We'll be off, never mind the storm." And with infinite sarcasm, he added, "You'll know where to find me, Inspector. At Castle Creedon." He gave a helpless half-laugh. "But . . . God knows, I didn't kill John Gwathney! Courts or no courts."

To Inspector O'Hare's amazement, Torrey Tunet said gravely, "I wouldn't doubt it" — and even as she looked at her watch, the door of the station opened.

50

A sprite of a man. Hatless, balding, with round brown eyes in a cheery face. His old-fashioned yellow oilskin was buckled high to his neck. He looked about, head tipped up like a bird jerkily questing.

"Here!" Torrey raised a hand and fluttered her fingers.

"Ah!" He came quickly down the side of the room, smiling. "So you're Ms. Tunet! Traffic slow, this rain, and I'm not an excellent driver. But I managed, obviously, because here I am!" His laugh showed small white teeth. He unbuckled the oilskin and shook it off. He wore a brown wool suit and tan shirt with a flowered tie.

Inspector O'Hare frowned impatiently at Ms. Tunet. His informal was over, it had revealed all. Tomorrow, the phone would ring, it would be Chief Superintendent O'Reilly calling from Dublin Castle congratulating him. "Egan," Chief Superintendent Emmet O'Reilly would say. "Egan —"

"Inspector," Ms. Tunet said, "this is Mr. Bendersford. He was kind enough to make the trip from Dublin. He'd dropped in at Gwathney Hall one day early in October."

Torrey glanced over at Megan O'Faolain beside Liam Caffrey. "Ms. O'Faolain may remember that visit as a pleasurable . . . But something happened that afternoon that is pertinent to John Gwathney's death. So . . ."

Exasperating. Inspector O'Hare frowned. But in a way, he owed her. And God only knew how long this thunderstorm would last, caging him with this gaggle of people on folding chairs. He looked around, met Sergeant Jimmy Bryson's gaze, shrugged, then nodded to Ms. Tunet.

"Thank you, Inspector." Ms. Tunet turned to Mr. Bendersford. "Tell us about that afternoon at Gwathney Hall, if you don't mind, Mr. Bendersford."

Mr. Bendersford had a kind, quiet voice, something a bit romantic in it, as he told of the afternoon he'd stopped at Gwathney Hall for John Gwathney to autograph one of his books for his nephew.

"So after a truly delectable lobster lunch," Mr. Bendersford recounted, "Gwathney showed me about the Hall. He had a few paintings he wanted me to see. I'm a dealer, in Dublin. In fact, about ten years ago, John Gwathney bought the Landseer through me. Two dogs. A fine Landseer, indeed.

"He took me into his study. Very private, no one allowed into his study except his assistant, Roger Flannery. I felt honored. He proudly showed me his favorite painting. It was on the wall between two windows. It was a Pissarro in a narrow gold frame. Lovely. On a tropical island, a dilapidated old mansion entangled in vines, a broken iron gate. As you may know, Camille Pissarro was born in the Virgin Islands, in 1830. He was a grown man before he came to Paris."

Mr. Bendersford paused. He sighed. "That painting in Gwathney's study. A gem of a painting — if it had been genuine, that is. But it was not."

Only the rain against the windowpanes. Then *"A forgery!"* someone breathed. Sheila Flaxton. "Oh, my!"

Mr. Bendersford shook his head. "No, ma'am. A forgery is a piece of work passed off as a previously undiscovered original. So, no. A *fake*, however, is a painting purporting to be an original." He smiled a sprightly smile at Sheila. "The Pissarro on John Gwathney's study wall was a fake."

Inspector O'Hare clasped his hands behind his back. What's this, what's *this?* Exasperating! Off on a tangent. A whole other bag of beans, nothing to do with his informal. A far cry from the business in hand, which was murder.

Mr. Bendersford, hands in his pockets, and rocking on his heels, sighed and shook his head. "You can imagine Gwathney's anger when I told him. Whoosh! Rage! Later, out on the steps of Gwathney Hall, as I was leaving, he said —"

" 'I'd like to strangle Clewes and Company!' " Winifred Moore said loudly, half out of her seat. Her hazel eyes in her square-jawed face, with its high russet color, were startled. "*That's* what John said!"

"Indeed! Indeed!" Mr. Bendersford nodded. "How do you do, again . . . Ms. Moore, if I recall?"

"You recall correctly, Mr. Bendersford." Winifred Moore looked past Mr. Bendersford at Torrey Tunet, who had taken something from the shoulder bag she had dropped on Inspector O'Hare's desk and was unrolling it. "What's *that?*"

Torrey further unrolled what appeared to be a worn canvas. She held it up. "The Pissarro."

Necks craned, Rosaleen O'Shea said, "What's it all *about?*" Roger Flannery said, "My God!" Blake Rossiter half-rose to see over Owen Thorpe's head. Willow Thorpe, back beside the soda machine, waved her white knitted cap at Ms. Tunet. Jasper Shaw ran a finger along his upper lip, suppressed a smile and regarded Ms. Tunet with a look of wonder.

Mr. Bendersford gave an exclamation of surprise. "Well, now! Yes, yes, indeed! The

Pissarro! That's it! That's the painting I saw in John Gwathney's studio. Quite, *quite* remarkable for a fake. I'm particularly a scholar of Pissarro. You know, he was not only a masterful painter, he was a teacher of Gauguin, Cassatt and Cézanne, among others." He stepped closer to the canvas, studying it, nodding. Then, peering closer, he frowned. "Wait a bit, if you don't mind, Ms. Tunet."

"Not at all." Torrey held the canvas taut. Mr. Bendersford fumbled in his breast pocket, took out a pair of spectacles, and put them on. Again he peered, again he frowned. "Hmm . . . It now has a brown stain, rusty-looking, on that left upper corner. Hmm . . . a smear, rather, that wasn't there when I saw it at Gwathney Hall." He peered even closer, moving his head from side to side. "Not paint. But more . . ." He looked up, rather like a startled rabbit. "Oh, my!"

Inspector O'Hare felt goose bumps.

51

Inspector O'Hare folded his arms. He looked grimly from the Pissarro to Mr. Bendersford to Ms. Torrey Tunet. She was rolling up the painting. O'Hare gave a sigh from the heart, never mind that the stain on the Pissarro could be anything and likely was . . . a bit of dirt caught in the process of the painting being rolled up, or . . . anything, an innocent bit of who knew what. But then, catching Sergeant Bryson's eye, he thought of his past association with Ms. Torrey Tunet and felt a chill. "What's all this about, Ms. Tunet? If you'll be so *good* as to . . . And exactly *how*, Ms. Tunet, did you come into possession of this painting?"

A hoot of a laugh, quickly suppressed, from back beside the soda machine. Willow Thorpe put a hand guiltily over her mouth.

Ms. Tunet pulled at a lock of hair that had escaped from her peacock bandanna. "I've always admired Pissarro." She looked at Mr. Bendersford. "From the Virgin Islands, was he? I never knew *that*." She looked back at Inspector O'Hare. "I was in John Gwathney's studio the day after he was killed. If there'd been a Pissarro on the wall, I'd have noticed it. It would have blown me away. But there was no Pissarro."

Ms. Tunet smiled at Mr. Bendersford. "Thanks to what you confirmed for me in our phone conversation this noon, I guessed that someone other than John Gwathney had removed the painting" — again she smiled at Mr. Bendersford — "and where the painting might be . . . if it hadn't been destroyed.

"So I commandeered Ms. Willow Thorpe and her motorbike." Here, one of Ms. Tunet's hands strayed to the seat of her jeans and she winced. "I found the painting rolled up in an umbrella stand. And I . . . uh, reclaimed it." Ms. Tunet looked over at Jasper Shaw. He was grinning. *Reclaimed,* as in "stole."

Inspector O'Hare's headache was becoming full-blown. "Found it *where,* Ms. Tunet? 'In an umbrella stand' is hardly sufficient —"

"Inspector O'Hare!" Mr. Bendersford broke in, his cheery face distressed. "Inspector, in fairness I ought to say that *I* am responsible for Ms. Tunet's ah . . . unusual activities. This noon, I was in my office in Dublin, lunching at my desk, my usual peanut-butter-and-olive on whole wheat, when I received that phone call from Ms. Tunet. She reminded me of my visit last September to Gwathney Hall and of John Gwathney's angry comment on discovering his Pissarro was a fake: 'I'd like to strangle Clewes and Company!' Ms. Tunet told me she thought she knew who Clewes and Company was, and she asked me if I could confirm it. I said yes, indeed. She asked me then, would I, an established, ah, authority in the art world, come to this investigation. She wanted me to appear and confirm who owned Clewes and Company."

The station was a frozen scene, the listeners immovable, not even the creak of a folding chair.

Mr. Bendersford continued. "So I told Ms. Tunet what John Gwathney had told me when I told him the Pissarro was a fake: that Clewes and Company is Blake Rossiter."

52

A stunned silence. Then Blake Rossiter laughed. "A thief and a schoolgirl! A fine pair! Invading my home! Stealing one of my paintings!" He raised his eyebrows at Inspector O'Hare. "Inspector! That's cause for legal action. And the garbled tale of Ms. Tunet! And the nonsense from that would-be Pissarro expert! *And,* need I point out that I was in Brussels when someone murdered John Gwathney?"

"Oh!" The exclamation came from Rosaleen O'Shea, and she got up so quickly from beside Blake Rossiter that her folding chair teetered. "But I *saw* you that afternoon! I was, uhh . . . wondering if you were, ah, *interested* in Colleen Healey and that's why you drove into Ballynagh through the back road that goes by the Healeys' and not through the village, what with her father being so crazy if anybody . . . So I . . . sort of bicycled up the back road, it being a lovely day, warmer than usual for the season." And Rosaleen backed up almost into Sergeant Bryson, who was standing along the wall.

Sergeant Bryson was feeling excited and a

little sick at Rosaleen's words. He had only his small police off-duty revolver, and if it had come to the revelation of Mr. Owen Thorpe of Castle Creedon as John Gwathney's killer, as he and Inspector O'Hare had expected, there would've been no problem; Owen Thorpe would've bowed his head, no violence, what with his wife and those twins right there.

But Blake Rossiter! Something in the glitter of Rossiter's narrowed eyes, and his fists that were slowly clenching, and his tensed body that might uncoil and spring . . . Sergeant Bryson reminded himself that he had never used the small handgun except in target practice.

Nevertheless, as Blake Rossiter sprang at Ms. Rosaleen O'Shea with the speed of a wildcat, Sergeant Bryson fired his off-duty revolver.

53

Thursday morning, eight o'clock at the police station, Sergeant Jimmy Bryson first thing made tea on the two-burner atop the soda machine. He'd have been at the station at half seven, but he'd been stopped several times on Butler Street by villagers congratulating him on his heroism yesterday afternoon in confronting Mr. Blake Rossiter, who now lay in hospital at Glasshill, thirty miles away, with a shoulder wound and something quite distasteful concerning his left lung. His legal prognosis was likely to be equally gloomy.

Sergeant Bryson had told his girlfriend, Hannah, about his dreadful confrontation with Rossiter at the police station informal. "He was two feet from me! He sprang like a wild beast! Teeth like fangs, and fingers like claws at Rosaleen's face!" To which Hannah had said, "Oh, indeed? Rosaleen O'Shea's face," and sniffed.

"Morning, Jimmy." Inspector O'Hare, with Nelson at his heels, came in just as the phone on his desk rang. Still in his police parka, and standing beside the desk, he picked it up. It was Gilbert Sanders in Forensics at Dublin Castle. "Yes . . . Yes,

Gilly." Listening, he was looking at Sergeant Bryson, who was holding a mug of tea, but not seeing him. "Yes. Right, as a matter of . . . Yes, I suspected . . . And the shell casing?"

He listened to Gilly's crackling voice with the Dublin accent from the Liberties quarter, tenements behind the Guinness works. But Sanders had fought his way up in the world. Smart. Forensics. "And the painting?" Listening, he said "Uh-huh" a couple of times more, nodding. Sergeant Bryson was watching him alertly. O'Hare said, "Thanks, Gilly. Hello to Francine."

He put down the phone and looked at Sergeant Bryson. "Is that tea yours or mine?"

"Yours." Bryson put the mug down on Inspector O'Hare's desk. O'Hare took a swallow of tea, then another. "The shell casing was fired from the shotgun that we found at Rossiter's lodge. The barrel of the shotgun itself had been spattered with blood and been wiped off."

Sergeant Bryson nodded; he felt years older than yesterday. "That shell casing — Hannah says that Kathleen from her Weight Watchers class says that at a dinner party at Megan O'Faolain's, she saw Blake Rossiter in the roped-off drawing room. He said he was looking for clues the Gardaí might've missed. Wanting to help Megan O'Faolain, he told Kathleen. Ho, ho!" Bryson blew out a breath and shook his head. "So . . . What about the smudge on the canvas? That the art fellow from Dublin —"

"Mr. Bendersford. The smudge. That, too. Might've been when Rossiter was running through the woods. Could've come off the shotgun."

Inspector O'Hare took off his parka and hung it on the stand. He came back and sat down at his desk. Yesterday, that final horror, as the ambulance sirened up to the police station, Rossiter lying there, agonized, raving. "A goat on a mountaintop, leaping . . . Insane! A madman when on drugs, worse when needing them! *I'll destroy you! I'll strangle your business. I'll ruin you!* He gloried in it! Wildness, rage, delight!" Then the white-jacketed attendant jumped down from the ambulance, and in a minute the injection, thank God.

O'Hare squeezed his forehead. During the night, he had done considerable thinking, lying on his back, hands behind his head, staring up at the ceiling. He said now, "That inventory, Jimmy. The Gwathney Hall inventory that Megan O'Faolain brought us the morning after John Gwathney was killed? Let me have a look at that again."

"Right, sir."

The inventory. Those three pages he'd had Sergeant Jimmy Bryson file away as useless in the investigation. "Not thievery," he had said to Megan O'Faolain. "A thief doesn't come armed with a twelve-gauge shotgun, too cumbersome. So, not thievery, Ms. O'Faolain." Remembering, he felt warmth at the back of his neck. He ran his forefinger slowly down the first page . . . then the second page. Halfway down the third page, he found it: "*Tropical Decay*, 1852, Camille Pissarro. 900,000 pounds. Clewes and Company, Dublin."

The fake. So, then, killing John Gwathney wasn't enough to keep Blake Rossiter safe from exposure. He had to take the painting. If the police checked the inventory, with robbery in mind, and found that a painting worth 900,000 pounds was missing, there'd be no way for the missing picture ever to be revealed as a fake.

O'Hare took a sip of lukewarm tea. Besides, if Gwathney's inheritors should decide to sell up Gwathney's paintings, better a painting missing from Gwathney's collection than a painting that might be revealed as a fake. A painting bought from Clewes and Company. Publicity! Clamor! Investigation!

"You want it hotted up?" Sergeant Bryson at his elbow, with the new glass carafe. O'Hare nodded. He watched the steam rise from his mug. "Rossiter should've destroyed the painting, Jimmy."

"Maybe he thought it was too good to waste, sir. Maybe he was thinking of selling it again." Carafe in hand, Bryson said, "That gold frame from the Pissarro? I'd guess, sir, that when we find it, it'll likely be framing one of Rossiter's other paintings at the lodge."

"No doubt." He watched Bryson return the carafe to the two-burner and switch the heat to low. Then he closed the Gwathney Hall inventory and sat gazing ahead, through the plate-glass window that fronted the station. He wanted to think of something ironic or philosophical, but nothing came to mind. A lorry drove past; across the street, the older Grogan sister was opening the Grogan Sisters Knitting Shop. Two schoolgirls walked past, wearing heavy jumpers and with their strapped books over their shoulders; one girl was bareheaded, the other wore a white knitted cap.

Inspector O'Hare momentarily stopped breathing. Then: "Thank God!"

"What's that, sir?"

O'Hare wiped cold sweat from his brow. "If she hadn't . . . If Ms. Torrey Tunet hadn't . . ." He stopped. Then: "Owen Thorpe."

Sergeant Bryson nodded. "Right, sir. Been thinking the same. What with the twins and his wife. They'd have gone through hell. Owen Thorpe all the time innocent, but wrecked if he came out of it alive. Guilt not proved, but sticking in folks' minds." Sergeant Bryson dug a dog biscuit out of the box and fed it to Nelson. At a sudden thought, he cast a sideways glance at Inspector O'Hare.

"Another thing, sir. Breaking and entering. Ms. Tunet and that Thorpe girl, Willow, could be arrested. And stealing the Pissarro from Rossiter's lodge. If anyone should care to press charges, sir?" He managed to suppress his grin.

54

They made love again in the early morning, frost still on the windowpanes, a weak sunlight beginning to filter through the trees on the east side of the cottage. Then Jasper said, "Did you get the raisins?" And at her drowsy nod he slid from under the down duvet that he'd bought her in Newry on the way down from Belfast, "to warm the cockles of your heart," he'd said, kissing her on the nose. "Not to mention your backside."

Creak of the oven door, delicious smell of raisin biscuits, sizzle of sausages in the pan. Cholesterol heaven, courtesy of her darling Jasper of the widening girth. It drew her out of bed.

Five minutes later, in jeans, brogues and an old red flannel shirt that had faded to pink, she came into the kitchen. She felt marvelously alive. Jasper had appeared at Inspector O'Hare's informal yesterday not only with John Gwathney's manuscript, conned out of a saucy-faced redhead on Pearse Street, but also with a rack of lamb and the news that he could stay four days.

"What's this?" Jasper, aproned, took something from the kitchen counter, shook flour off it and held it up. "Were you trying to make biscuits again? This was in the flour bin." He was grinning.

She took it from him. A small, tawny-colored address book. She riffled slowly through the pages. There: Owen Thorpe, Castle Creedon, Baltimore, Cork.

She giggled. "In the flour bin! So Roger Flannery only stole the journal back from me. The journal was what he mostly cared about, anyway. He stole it because —"

"Because he couldn't read Greek?"

Torrey nodded. "He must've been afraid it would reveal that John Gwathney was eager to publish *The Raid of Baltimore*, not burn it." She followed Jasper to the kitchen table, sat down and watched him put two sausages onto her plate and four onto his own. "God! Poor Flannery! There he was, *literally*, poor. So, tempted to swipe the manuscript and blackmail the Thorpes."

Jasper set down the basket of biscuits and poured their tea. "Right. I did a bit of investigating, known in *your* lexicon as 'snooping.' Flannery: Years of driving a beat-up old Nissan, wearing shirts with frayed cuffs, shoes with run-down heels, and picking butts out of ashtrays. Due, doubtless to: cost of leg surgery for Ms. Cherry Dugan, involving three operations; one divorce for Ms. Cherry Dugan; weekly voice-coach lessons for aspiring singer Ms. Cherry Dugan, who, according to my sources — both successful guitarists — is 'a luv, man, with a knock-out voice, she'll make it, man, it's in the cards.' "

"That's marvelous . . . I'm wondering, Jasper. After Flannery inherited the Landseer and got so rich, d'you suppose he *really* would've gone ahead and tried to blackmail Owen Thorpe?"

Jasper cut into a sausage. "Maybe, maybe not. But he's damned lucky O'Hare's informal exposed him before he could even try it. Thus, my dear lass, Flannery's life of crime never really got off the ground. If it had, and misfired along the way, he might even have lost Ms. Cherry Dugan."

At Gwathney Hall, Megan O'Faolain came into John Gwathney's study. It was noon, the sun shone through the tall arched windows. It was the first time she had been able to bring herself to enter this so private workroom since John Gwathney's death. There was still a stale smell of tobacco, though John Gwathney had seldom smoked. It was chilly and Megan shivered. She wore a rust-colored wool skirt and a beige turtleneck sweater. Her dark hair was cupped behind her ears. She walked to the windows and looked out at the mountains. Then she sighed, turned, came back toward the door and stopped before what she had come into the study to see: the snapshots on the wall, in their black frames, the photographs of John Gwathney in those earlier days. Here was John Gwathney as he'd been when he'd first ducked out of the rain and into that bare weaver's shop where she had already packed up to leave Ballynagh.

Back then. Back when she had loved him, when he'd been the John Gwathney of these photos. Hands clasped behind her back, she gazed at the snapshots: John, the way he had been, keen-eyed, writing it all down in desert tents, in snow-swept huts, in caravansaries, recording it on cassettes, photographing it, turning it into books.

"Megan?" Liam in the study doorway. "I saw you come up. You're all right?" His voice was edgy, his brows drawn into a frown.

She smiled at him, remembering how it had been summer when she'd begun to visit the pottery shop, and how one day it had been swelteringly hot, and unthinkingly she had rolled up her shirtsleeves and he had seen the yellow-edged dark bruise. When he learned, when she finally confessed, he had barely contained his anger, his rage at John Gwathney. *"I'd like to kill him!"* And later, for a brief, terrible moment, she had wondered, in horror . . .

"I'm fine. I just came in here to see" — she gestured at the snapshots — "back *then*."

Back then. Back before the drugs and abuse

and her stubborn attempts to help him. Back before, finally, she had known that whether she could get help for him or not, she was going to leave him. She had known that even before the day she had happened into the pottery shop.

"Yes . . . well." Liam nodded.

Megan smiled at him, thinking, An odd thing — he looks younger since John Gwathney's death. He was, in fact, two years younger than her, with a long-ago failed boyhood marriage behind him. They were still friends, Liam and his ex-wife, that confused girl who had discovered herself to be a lover of women. She was young, rich and titled, so the scandal sheets had gone wild with the story when she took up with a woman lover. Inspector O'Hare, who had certainly been getting on to the Glasgow police about Liam Caffrey's past, would finally have revived the scandal. But these days, would anyone really have cared? Once a year, Liam and his ex-wife dined together, had champagne and laughed about their year-long marriage.

"Look over there," Megan said, looking past his shoulder.

Liam turned, looked, then frowned. "What? I don't . . ."

"The wall, between the windows." She was gazing at the faint rectangular darker patch on the eighteenth-century scrolled wallpaper. It was just to the right of the desk, where,

John Gwathney, at work, could look up and contemplate whatever might have been there.

"The Pissarro?" Liam asked.

Megan nodded.

Willow and Buddy left Castle Creedon by the terrace doors. They went down the broad half-circle of stone steps and headed across the dry grass for the stables. It was eleven in the morning and sunny, but a brisk wind was blowing. They walked with their hands in the pockets of their jackets, shoulders hunched. Buddy was bareheaded, Willow wore her white knitted cap.

It was warmer in the stable, and when they'd lit a cigarette each they sat on the wooden bench outside of Flashback's stall. "Which of them is the 'man' in it?" Buddy said, "the one with that Australian outback hat? Most likely."

"Hard to tell." Willow contemplated her cigarette. "Sex is different with different ones." She took a deep breath of the warm stable smell. "Poor darling Mummy and Daddy! They must have been in agony after that second visit from John Gwathney. Afraid we were going to lose Creedon."

"That Inspector O'Hare," Buddy said. "Pa could've lost more than Creedon. Jesus! It was mighty close!"

Willow nodded. "I guess Ms. Tunet has a really sore behind."

Buddy said, "Algerian pirates, sixteen-thirty-one. That's over three hundred and fifty years ago. And then the crummy old hairbrush. Weird." Behind him, Flashback whinnied and kicked the side of her stall.

Willow put out her cigarette on the sole of her left brogue. "Like that ancient body of a man found in a bog in Scotland last year? Really *ancient*. Turned out, from the DNA, to be an ancestor of a half dozen Scotsmen in Edinburgh. One of them was in last summer's PGA Scottish Region's golf tournament at Gleneagles."

Buddy stood up and put the pack of cigarettes back in the box. "You take Flashback, I'll ride Jenny."

"Hmm?" Willow's very blue eyes had a concentrated look; she was somewhere else. "I have a certain facility for languages. I could get about, travel. Did you see Ms. Tunet's watch? It has the date, day and world time-sweep."

Buddy said, "Shall we try hitting up Pa for an increase in our allowance? He should be in a pretty affluent mood."

55

It was after dinner, the pork roast with apples had been heavenly. Chocolate sorbet-and-banana dessert. The peat fire kept the cottage warm. Torrey wore only a T-shirt with her jeans. Jasper was in his abominable horizontally striped blue-and-white cotton sweater. They still sat at the kitchen table, the teapot on a hot plate.

"A bit of history for you," Jasper said. "I poked around an archive or two, not my field. But anything you're involved in captures my interest. Here's this." He put something down beside Torrey's teacup.

Torrey picked it up. It was a photocopy of a letter. Exquisite, old-style handwriting. It bore a crest of crossed swords, with a rose between the hilts.

My dear cousin Sarah,

We give thanks to God that we were not among the kidnapped. We have lived through the horror of our friends' loss, and nightmares of their fate there in Africa. We will at once remove to Longford, far from this dangerous coast. We hope never to see the sea again, or to smell salt air. Our prayers and sadness go to Celia and Desmond Creedon and their little Annabel, kidnapped from our shores by those Barbary pirates. Their fate is something we dread to imagine. You will hear from us, once we are settled in Longford.

Your loving cousin,
Louise.
Baltimore, Co. Cork.
August 12, 1631

For some minutes there was only the ticking of the old wall clock that Torrey had found at a tag sale. Then Torrey said,

"But we *do* know little Annabel's fate! At least that. It was in John Gwathney's journal . . . What he learned from the monastery's old records: The child lacking a last finger was one of three children the monastery sold to villagers in the nearby Berber village. Only forty years ago, that village was attacked and pillaged by brigands from the Aurès Mountains. A handful of the villagers escaped through the desert to the monastery. One of them, the only one of his family to remain alive, stayed on as gatekeeper at the monastery, and according to the journal, 'is much valued.'" Torrey paused. "I expect it's all in John Gwathney's manuscript."

Jasper's eyebrows rose and he whistled softly under his breath. "John Gwathney, investigative reporter."

"Hmm?" Torrey was looking dreamily off

into space. "I keep wondering . . . about how somewhere there are descendants of the people kidnapped from Baltimore. Living in Algeria . . . or nearby Tunisia . . . or Morocco . . . ."

"Let it go," Jasper said. "Let it go."

In the morning, toward noon, she went with Jasper past the pond and through the hedge to the Jaguar parked at the side of the access road. This time he'd be going south, destination known only to someone at a desk at the *Independent* in Dublin. A cold wind was blowing, low clouds obscured the tops of the surrounding mountains, mist lay in tattered layers across the hills. Shivery weather; barns would be dank, animals huddled within, hooves stamping, breath steaming.

In her parka, Torrey stood beside the car, the window wound down. Jasper reached out an arm and drew her head close and kissed her cold nose. "E-mail me from Portugal, right? And bring back some of those dried Portuguese sausages. I have a recipe waiting. And . . ." In his long Irish face, his nostrils twitched. "Pray for Irish political peace."

Jasper gone, she went back through the hedge. The cold wind made her eyes tear. There was a thin-looking sheet of ice on the pond as she went past it to the cottage. It would be warm in Portugal. In a week? Two weeks? She should call Myra Schwartz at Interpreters International. What time was it in Boston?

Indoors, the phone was ringing, then a voice, "Torrey? It's Myra in —"

She ran across the room and snatched up the phone. "Myra! I'm here! I'm here!"

"Well, now, honey bunch, *hello*. Can you believe it? Portugal *again* off! But a diplomatic brouhaha in Greece, I'm tickled to say. So, Greece. I've already booked you a room at the Acropolis Palace in Athens. Near the *plaka, and* with a view of that temple with the Vestal Virgins. Sunday through Thursday . . . Oh, wait! I'm just looking at your . . . Greek *is* one of your languages, isn't it? I just took it for . . . Anyway, Greek is, isn't it?"

Torrey said, "Yes, Myra, it is." It is *now*.

Whistling under her breath, she packed the sleeveless black dress, the dangling jet earrings, the sandals and walking shoes and the rest on the list pasted inside her suitcase. Lastly, she packed the Greek dictionary and grammar.

Then, standing in the fireplace kitchen, she unwrapped a chocolate bar, bit off a piece and stood pensively looking about at the hutch under the wall clock, at her desk in the alcove and at the shabby old couch she'd meant to finish slipcovering with the pea-green corduroy she'd bought over a year ago. But then: A child alone on a dark street . . .

She finished the chocolate bar. She stood a

moment frowning, biting a fingernail. Then she tied the peacock scarf around her head as a bandanna, put on her parka and left the cottage.

It was just twelve noon. At O'Malley's Pub she'd find Michael McIntyre of the wild white thicket of hair and tales of his seafaring days along the coast of North Africa, so long after those Barbary Coast pirate days, but perhaps holding a whiff of the past.

She would let go, of course, finally. "Let it go," as Jasper had said. And yes, she would. But slowly.